ABOUT THE AUTHOR

George G. Gilman was born in 1936 in what was then a small village east of London. He attended local schools until the age of fifteen. Upon leaving school he abandoned all earlier ambitions and decided to become a professional writer, with strong leanings towards the mystery novel. He wrote short stories and books during evenings, lunch hours, at weekends, and on the time of various employers while he worked for an international newsagency, a film company, a weekly book-trade magazine and the Royal Air Force.

His first short (love) story was published when he was sixteen and the first (mystery) novel ten years later. He has been a full-time writer since 1970, writing mostly Westerns which have been translated into a dozen languages and have sold in excess of 16 million copies. He is married and lives on the Dorset coast, which is as far west as he intends to move right now.

Terror Town

George G. Gilman

NEW ENGLISH LIBRARY
Hodder and Stoughton

for
R. M.
Who knows how wild it
really can get out west

A New English Library
Original Publication, 1988

Copyright © 1988 by
George G. Gilman

First published in
Great Britain in 1988
by New English
Library Paperbacks

British Library C.I.P.

Gilman, George G., *1936–*
Terror town.
Rn: Terry Harknett
I. Title
823'.914[F]

ISBN 0-450-43110-X

*The characters and situations in
this book are entirely imaginary
and bear no relation to any real
person or actual happening.*

Printed and bound in Great
Britain for Hodder and Stoughton
Paperbacks, a division of Hodder
and Stoughton Ltd., Mill Road,
Dunton Green, Sevenoaks, Kent
TN13 2YA (Editorial Office: 47
Bedford Square, London, WC1B
3DP) by Richard Clay,
Bungay, Suffolk.

1

It seemed like the rain did not let up all night. And when the wind from the north west stopped gusting down out of the Cascade Mountains every now and then the noise level fell hardly at all. For the sound of rushing water in the swollen creeks took its place.

But despite the Oregon storm that raged hour after hour, Edge stayed dry and slept pretty well in a deep cleft at the base of a granite escarpment beside the trail into Winton.

Maybe not as well as if he had headed into town, taken a room at the Winton Hotel. But he was still better than ten miles south east of town when the rainstorm was unleashed with violent suddenness. And the gaping hole at the base of the wall of rock offered a convenient place to shelter for the half-breed and his roan gelding.

When, after an hour, the wind-driven rain showed no sign of easing, he elected to spend the rest of the night here in the dry, instead of getting sodden through to the skin by riding to Winton—a town where he had no pressing need to be, anyway. It just happened to be on an intersection of the trail he was riding and one that reached down into California toward his ultimate destination.

Damnit, that wasn't right!

Just the first notion to enter his head as he came awake for the sixth or seventh time since he bedded down in the total darkness of full night.

This time, though, it was not an obtrusive sound of the storm which disturbed him, nudged him to the brink of awareness and held him there just a moment before he sank back into deep, untroubled sleep.

Doubtless dreamt in the depths of his subconscious, he

7

realised, as he now came fully awake, snapped open his eyes to the gloomy grey light of the rain-filled dawn: felt fully rested.

He scowled at the weather that veiled this soaked stretch of the trail which was flanked to the north by the fifty-feet-high cliff, to the south by a forest of spruce and pine and an occasional lone oak or elm. And told himself, as he folded up from under his blankets, let go his loose grip around the frame of the Winchester that had shared his bed, it was simply the depressing sights and sounds of the incessant rain which triggered his ill humour at the instant of waking.

But as he began preparations to leave the night camp he knew he was lying to himself. Then the fact he should enter into such a futile mental exercise served to replace depression with irritation.

Just because Adam Steele had set himself up in business as a horse rancher in the Providence River Valley, somewhere down in California. Which was where the trail that ran south from the crossroad town of Winton, Oregon went to.

So he must have been having some kind of dream about the Virginian and his lousy horse ranch! But he was damned if he was going to let a feeling triggered by his subconscious, a kind of feeling dangerously close to envy, influence him while he was awake!

His horse, which had shared the spacious cave-like hole in the rock wall with him, vented a nostril-flaring snort as he tossed and swung his head. Looked balefully from the weather toward Edge and saw—maybe registered the meaning in his equine mind—that the man was rolling up his blankets and so had no intention of delaying the start for a cup of coffee and a shave. That would have allowed rider and mount awhile longer to keep dry in the shelter.

'Yeah, I know how you feel, boy,' Edge muttered as his mood started to lighten. To an extent so he could show a grin, albeit lacking in warmth, and inject a tone of wry humour into his voice. 'Around me it seems like it never does rain but it pours. Still, they do say there's worse trouble at sea, uh?'

The horse snorted less forcefully, looking morosely out at

8

the teeming rain once more. And Edge completed tying the bedroll, growled in a tone to match the grim look in the animal's bulging eyes:

'Sure, but maybe not so much water as there is in Oregon.'

The hobbled horse showed no further interest in continuing the conversation: seemed to convey as the saddle was swung over his back, the cinch was fastened and the accoutrements were hung in place, he was as aggrieved at his rider as the weather.

Then, when there were just the hobbles to be removed from the gelding's forelegs, Edge did delay the departure. Took the makings from a shirt pocket and rolled a cigarette. Slanted it from the corner of his mouth, struck a match on the stock of his rifle which jutted from the forward-hung boot on the right side of the saddle.

He took his time smoking the cigarette, because it looked like this weather could keep up for a long time, which meant he was unlikely to get the chance of another smoke until he reached Winton.

Tobacco and the occasional shot of rye were the only luxuries Edge missed when circumstances caused him to be deprived of them. All other hardships he had learned to accept: did not allow himself to be concerned whenever he was denied them.

There had been much hardship and deprivation during the more than forty years of his life: that could be readily judged by anyone with an ounce of perception if they gave this man more than a passing glance. And most people did spare him more than the casual attention they might give to most strangers. For he had those kinds of looks, that brand of demeanour which marked him out as different from the herd.

He was a tall, lean man of middle years: stood something over six feet two inches tall and weighed an evenly-distributed, solidly-fleshed two hundred and some pounds. It was obvious he had the blood of two races running through his veins, though there was no way to recognise it was his father who had been Mexican, his mother from Scandinavia. Both parents were American by adoption, Edge by his birth on a small farmstead in Iowa.

In recent years it seemed that as he grew older only the light blueness of his permanently-narrowed hooded eyes marked him as a half-breed. For the burnish of his skin, deeply lined by the harsh experiences of so much of his life, stained by the elements on the already dark hue of his Mexican heritage, had stressed the Latin bloodline with increasing emphasis as the years passed. Likewise, the basic structure of his lean features with high cheekbones, hooked nose and wide, thin-lipped mouth had seemed to take on a more decidedly Mexican cast. And this impression was furthered by the way he wore an underplayed moustache that curved down to either side of his mouth.

But no more did the jet blackness of his hair, long enough to brush his shoulders and fringe the nape of his neck, strongly indicate his part Mexican parentage. For these days it was not so lushly thick, and there were distinct strands of grey mingled with it.

Always, though, his slitted and glinting blue eyes revealed that second bloodline. Eyes that were the predominant feature of the kind of strong face atop the kind of powerful frame that could never make him one of the average crowd. Eyes, perversely inherited from the most gentle of women, that warned of the latent cruelty beneath the surface of the man: suggested he could be brutal at the least provocation, was totally lacking in compassion for anything—anybody—he did not love.

And it was difficult to imagine a man such as this ever experiencing such a tender emotion as love.

If there were many pointers to his character in his physical characteristics, there was nothing about the manner of his dress that showed him to be different from other drifting saddletramps. Riding the trails in search of casual work to raise money for the next shot of whiskey, poke of tobacco, easy woman, or more essential supplies for himself and his horse.

He wore a dark-hued hat, kerchief, shirt, pants and spurless boots. The clothing and its colour not selected for any effect it might have on his appearance, but because the outfit was hard wearing and offered the best deal available at the time he bought it.

10

If there was one seeming affectation about the garb of the man, it was the beaded thong that encircled his throat: mostly was concealed under the kerchief. Once, the beads had been brightly coloured, but time had faded them to dullness. Not that they had ever been intended for ornamentation as far as Edge was concerned. It was just that when, as a cavalry officer in the Union army, he had acquired the circlet of beads to which was attached a pouch containing a straight razor, that had been their form.

Just occasionally he had need to use the razor in the neck pouch for purposes other than shaving. Mostly, though, he shaved with it. And if there was need of a weapon for whatever purpose, he employed the Frontier Colt he carried in the holster tied down to his right thigh. Or the Winchester repeater that had shared his bed, now was stowed in the boot on the saddle.

The rain continued to beat down, the wind to gust, while he stood in the cave. Smoked the cigarette. Sometimes removed it from the corner of his mouth and ran the back of a hand raspingly over the bristles on his jaw. More often remained unmoving: used the time to clear his mind of the clutter of unwanted notions.

But he did not try to achieve this by imposing excuses for why he had come up to Oregon for a specific purpose after he left Munro over in Colorado.

He was just drifting.

Financed by what was left of a stake comprised of the reward money he unwittingly but justly earned out of some violent trouble that got started in the town of San Cristobel, way down south in the Territory of Arizona.

So, if he really was so damn eager to cast an intrigued eye over the kind of spread Adam Steele had gotten for himself, judge the style of life the Virginian was leading in the Californian valley, why had he taken such a wide swing across the western states and territories?

So, damnit, he was just doing what he'd always done!

Drifting like the loner he was. Doing his level best to avoid trouble. Not always succeeding, when fate dictated he should meet up with other people!

From force of habit he crushed out the embers of the

11

cigarette before he arced the butt through the teeming rain. Was about to stoop and free the gelding from the hobbles when he heard a sound in the storm that was not caused by the weather. A moment later recognised galloping hooves splashing along the trail that the rain had turned into a quagmire.

The gelding's equine senses told him of the nearness of one of its own kind and Edge reached out a hand to run the palm gently over the animal's muzzle. Like all his earlier mounts, the roan had been schooled to understand that the gesture meant he should stay calm and quiet: reassured there was nothing to be concerned about.

A few seconds after he first heard the new sound in the slightly brightening morning, it ended. But this had been long enough for Edge to have gotten a bearing on it. He knew the rider was approaching from the direction of Winton.

He completed unhobbling the horse and then drew back into the darkness at the rear of the cave. The trail ran immediately across the front of the cleft in the wall of rock, was just a dozen feet wide. And he didn't want to startle the lone rider, delay him in what was obviously an urgent mission, judging from his speed through such bad weather. More importantly to the half-breed, he had no desire to delay his own start for any longer than was necessary.

But the sounds of the rain and the wind in the timber remained uninterrupted by galloping hooves, and nobody raced a horse across the mouth of the cave within the next fifteen seconds or so.

Edge moved forward into the murky daylight of dawn again, a hand on the gelding's bridle. Halted on the cave's threshold as a hammering sound began. Metal on metal: a hammer striking a nailhead, maybe. More than one nailhead, he decided. This new sound came from the west again. No more than a couple of hundred feet, which was far enough so the hammering man could not be seen by the half-breed.

Then just the familiar sounds of the storm filled the early morning again. But Edge's sense that he was not alone in this piece of rain sodden Oregon timber country remained strong; though in such a situation there was no indication of hostility, innocent indifference or anything in between. He simply knew there was somebody else close by. Why he was there and what he—or she?—was doing could have nothing to do with Edge, a stranger in these parts.

Since he wanted to keep it this way, he remained where he was, peering into the west, listening for further sounds not caused by the elements. Ready to duck back into the depths of the cave's interior should the man remount, continue to gallop eastward.

Then he heard a whinny, just as the wind gusted a break in the curtain of rain and he glimpsed a figure as it swung smoothly up astride a horse. A figure wearing a shiny black slicker, thudding into the saddle on a dark-coloured horse.

A moment later rain veiled the scene again, the horse snorted and lunged into an immediate gallop. Back the way it had come, so that soon the sound of hooves splashing along the mire-like trail was lost behind the beat of rain and the whine of the wind.

And Edge was left feeling curiously intrigued as he draped a slicker over his shoulders, then led his horse by the reins out into the storm.

After fifty or sixty paces, his booted feet sinking ankle-deep into the mud from which it was hard work to withdraw them, he was close enough to confirm what he thought he had seen: that startling feature of the scene that had caused him to pay such scant attention to the horse and rider during the momentary gap opened up in the rain. He had, in fact, seen exactly what he thought he did: a noosed length of rope did hang, swinging in the gusting wind, from the lowest branch of an oak tree that was the only one of its kind growing among the pines and spruce in the immediate area. This rope so placed that it dangled down over the centre of the trail. Not high enough off the ground to string up anyone except a dwarf or a small child. Low enough so it could not be missed by anyone moving on the trail, astride a horse, riding a wagon or walking.

Now Edge's impassive-faced attention was captured by two flyers nailed to the trunk of the oak. And he detoured around the hanging rope, got close enough to read them.

One had been torn and tattered by the elements for some time: would have been difficult to read before the night of incessant rain almost disintegrated it. It was almost illegible, but the half-breed did manage to make out it was a playbill. Advertising some kind of entertainment that was to be held—more likely had already been staged—at the Winton Theatre. It had been commercially printed in three colours.

The more recent notice, the nails Edge heard being hammered in holding it securely at all four corners, was on thick card. Its red-painted lettering in block capitals was still clearly legible, although the rain was starting to darken the once white background. The flyer proclaimed:

CURLY DIDN'T DO IT
BUT HE CAN'T BE BROUGHT BACK

Edge suddenly became aware of another horse on the trail, this one approaching from the east and making less haste than the rider who left the message that was clear to Edge in principle but not in particular.

This second horse was in the traces of a light rig, and this time Edge did not attempt to remain out of sight. He stayed beside the oak tree with its hanging noose and starkly stated message. For no other reason than he felt he had no call to avoid other travellers on this length of public Oregon trail.

He peered eastward and was indifferently conscious that he probably looked a somewhat sinister figure in the rain against the backdrop of the gruesome noosed rope hanging from the tree branch.

Then the driver of the leather-roofed, window-sided buggy brought the rig to an abrupt halt as soon as he drove within sight of the scene under the oak. The vehicle was open fronted and Edge saw a hurried movement within the double-seated interior. Sensed the driver's fear as he lifted a hand from under his slicker, tipped his hat and greeted evenly:

'I'm not going to say good morning in weather like this is, feller.' He had used his left hand to touch the brim of his Stetson. Moved his right to hover close to his holstered Colt as he added; 'Want to tell you, it'll be a short one if you don't move your hand away from the rifle.'

The other man's elegantly white gloved right hand was

14

snatched back from where it had curled around the frame of a Winchester wedged into a corner of the seat.

'My God, what does that mean, sir?'

The man, who did not sound young, rasped the question in a tone that suggested his throat was constricted by a brand of fear deep enough to verge on terror. Edge replied evenly:

'That you shouldn't aim a gun at me unless you plan to kill me. I give folks the one warning.'

'I...'

'Mistakes happen. That one only once.'

'What?' the man in the buggy spluttered. Shook his head vigorously. 'Oh, no. I didn't mean...' Now irritable impatience displaced fear. 'I was referring to the meaning of the noose hanging from the tree. Is that your doing, sir?'

Edge directed a sidelong glance at the noosed rope, swung up into the saddle before he answered. 'Glad to say I'm a stranger in these parts. I don't know what it means, and I don't want to know.'

'But surely... The fact that you are here... You had dismounted and——'

Edge pointed with a hooked thumb, broke in: 'There's a message nailed to the tree. Claims somebody named Curly didn't do something I'd guess he was hanged for.'

When the half-breed spoke the name, the man in the buggy caught his breath. Finally let it out in a strangled cry after Edge finished giving his interpretation of the sign.

'Curly was the nickname of John Grady, mister,' he said huskily. 'It was I who sentenced young Grady to be executed for murder. Charles C. Benedict, circuit judge.'

'It's a job somebody has to do,' Edge said flatly, tugged on the reins to turn his gelding in the direction of Winton.

'You spoke of mistakes just now,' Benedict reminded morosely. 'What if a fatal one was made? It certainly seems as if somebody thinks young Grady was hanged for a murder he did not commit.'

'Yeah, Judge,' Edge said, heeled the gelding forward at a slow walk through the clinging mud. 'I guess we both got the message.'

2

Judge Charles C. Benedict seemed to be too shaken to move a muscle as he reflected upon the wrongful hanging and Edge started to ride unhurriedly westward. Then, with a short cry of alarm that was loud enough to penetrate the sounds of the rain and wind, the hooves and wheels in the mud, he lurched his rig in the wake of the half-breed, soon came up alongside the horseback rider.

'Do you have any objection if we travel to Winton together, sir?'

'It's where I'm headed, Judge.'

'You aren't concerned to be in the company of a man singled out by Grady's...' He couldn't think of what he had been singled out for: or suddenly discovered he could not express his dread of words.

Edge told him: 'If somebody wanted to do worse than scare you for now, Judge, I figure he'd have done it in the cover of the storm. Instead of getting himself soaked taking all that trouble with the noose and the notice. No, I'm not concerned.'

'I appreciate it, sir.' He swallowed hard and struck a match in the shelter of the roof and sides of the buggy, touched the flame to the tip of a large cigar. 'Both for your company and your reassuring thought on the macabre scene back there. You are, of course, absolutely correct. Fletcher Grady simply wants to unnerve me. Make me feel even worse than I do about the possible miscarriage of justice that claimed the life of his son.'

In the light of the flaring match as it was held to the end of the cigar, Edge was able to see that the man who set up the sinister tableau at the oak tree had succeeded in doing just that. Benedict had been badly scared and continued to suffer from the effects of being shaken to his nerve endings as he sucked in a stream of smoke, held it in his lungs for several tense seconds, then allowed it out through his nostrils with a soft sighing sound.

Although he had been so afraid at first sight of Edge beside the noosed rope, the timbre of his opening words had given an accurate pointer to his age. He was past sixty, maybe closer to seventy.

He had a round, fleshy face, much of it concealed by long, broad sidewhiskers that met in a moustache but did not join to form a beard beneath his thick, slightly protruding lips. This hair was silvery white, but the steeply arched eyebrows over his small eyes flanking the prominent bridge of his nose were dark.

His build was bulky: but the clothing he wore against the damp chill of the new day's weather maybe made him look heavier than he was. The Stetson, topcoat, gloves and the cravat between the velvet lapels of the coat were all of fine quality. So was the cut-under buggy he drove and the horse in its traces: muddied from travel, but not so much of it completed this morning. The chestnut gelding had not come far after a night's rest. Likewise the judge had not been long out of a bed in which he had slept well.

Edge thought that when the man presided in a court of law, in undisputed command of the proceedings amid the trappings of the legal system, Judge Charles C. Benedict was doubtless an awe-inspiring figure deserving of respect from whoever had business in his courtroom. Now, in the rain-sodden early morning, having just suffered a severe shock, he looked and sounded pathetic in his fear as he made it clear he considered talk could calm his jangling nerves.

'It happened three months ago, sir,' he opened huskily.

'What did, Judge?' Edge asked absently, relishing the aroma of Benedict's expensive tobacco. Which seemed to go some way toward combatting the chilling dampness of the weather as the wind slackened, which eased the force of the rain beating into his face.

'The trial and execution of John Grady, Mr...?' He

17

sounded disgruntled: as a judge he was obviously a man used to having the undivided attention of his listeners.

'The name's Edge.'

'Good. Mr Edge. Yes, I tried John Grady during my last visit to Winton. Mostly I hold court in the towns on my circuit approximately every quarter. There are just the ten communities where court is held, but I have to travel widely. For my jurisdiction reaches from the Californian border north to the town of Bend. And stretches from the Catlow Rim to the east into these foothills of the Cascade Mountains.'

Edge excused his ignorance of the area of which Benedict spoke. 'Like I said, Judge, I'm a stranger in this part of the country. Heard in Fort Rock that from Winton I can pick up a trail south to California. And if I feel the need, I can spend some time for not too much money at the Winton Hotel.'

The elderly man in the buggy was now enthusiastically eager to talk on a subject so far divorced from the case of a man he perhaps unjustly sentenced to death. 'You were correctly informed sir. The town of Winton is able to supply much of what a man needs in the way of essentials and creature comforts. And the Henderson's hotel is one of the finest on my circuit, in my opinion.'

'Storm keep you from making it to the hotel last night, Judge?'

It was just a question, asked out of mild curiosity. But it disconcerted Benedict, suddenly drained his enthusiasm.'

'What? Oh, yes... Well, I don't often stay at the Winton Hotel any more, Mr Edge. I stay with an old friend at a farm in the hills to the south of the trail. When a man travels so much as I have to, it's a blessed relief to enjoy the domestic hospitality of friends. Rather than the comfort but somehow impersonal benefits of a hotel, I find?'

'Guess I can understand that,' Edge responded to the implied query as the sweet fragrance of tobacco smoke got stronger: the judge obviously doing a great deal of rapid inhaling and exhaling—maybe just to get the cigar drawing evenly again after he had neglected it. Or while he struggled to pick up the threads of what he had been saying before he allowed himself to be sidetracked on to a subject that had suddenly lost its appeal. Finally he announced:

'I was saying, Mr Edge!' The irritation of impatience had crept into his tone again.

Almost always when he travelled open trails, rode town streets, or was even in a room with other people, the half-breed channelled part of his attention to his surroundings, remained constantly alert to spot the unexpected before it happened. Most of the time, whatever effort this required seemed to be wasted: when nothing untoward happened. But there had been occasions, more than he chose to recall, when his habitual surveillance had saved his life. So he had good cause not to consider it was a wasteful exercise. And anyway, because it had become a habit, a custom he had developed early and honed down the dangerous years, it required a little conscious effort. Until he saw, or sensed, sign of an imminent threat.

He was not infallible: particularly in circumstances when there was no good reason for a need to stay alert to potential danger. But he never blamed himself for this after an impulse to rage was suppressed. Neither did he ever excuse himself to anyone who resented his lack of wholehearted attention to them.

'You were saying?' he echoed, peered into the interior of the buggy.

Now the fully broken dawn had become so much brighter, he could see the network of wrinkles and purple veins that tracked across the judge's face above the white whiskers. Saw the hirsute features clearly enough to witness the man's change of expression: this as Benedict met the level gaze of the narrowed, ice-blue eyes, did not like the impassive expression on Edge's unshaven face.

'Oh, I thought I had failed to hold your interest, Mr Edge,' the judge almost stuttered.

The half-breed told him: 'If you'd done that, Judge, either I'd be gone or I'd have told you to shut up.'

Benedict suddenly found the cigar not to his liking, snatched it from between his thick lips and hurled it violently away, snapped: 'You don't mince your words, do you, sir?'

Edge shrugged. 'I'm the way I am, Judge. You don't like it, I've got no reason to ride into town with you.'

Benedict continued to express his irritation for a few more moments. Then he suppressed it with a throaty sound he probably reserved usually for dismissing an obviously false piece of evidence presented in his court. Then he said grimly:

'It had all the hallmarks of a classic open and shut case—as we of the legal calling refer to them. A travelling theatre company was staging an entertainment in the Winston Colliseum. One of the performers was a pretty young woman named Teresa Ward, who had apparently turned quite a few heads in Winton. Some of which should not have been turned. Married men, you understand?'

'I guess I do,' Edge answered, prepared to go this far to demonstrate to the still suspicious judge that he was listening while he continued to remain alert to other aspects of his surroundings.

Since they had moved beyond where the escarpment petered out, the timber-flanked trail had started to climb in a series of long and gentle curves. Which the horses would have found little more demanding than the flat had it not been for the clinging mud.

'This did have a bearing on the case,' Benedict went on quickly, like he was anxious to dispense with the issue. 'The bare facts of the matter are that on the final night of the company's engagement in town, Miss Ward failed to appear at the theatre. And the immediate reaction among certain sections of the community was that she had run off with one of the local men who had been so taken with her. But the theatre people would have no truck with that suggestion. Miss Ward, it seemed, always stirred up such interest in towns wherever performances were staged. She invariably encouraged such attention, but never took the men seriously.'

The judge made a sound of disgusted disapproval with such behaviour. 'The following morning, after it was established none of the local men had left, the body of Miss Ward was discovered. She had been stripped naked, raped and strangled with a piece of her own intimate underclothing. It was clear somebody had objected in the strongest possible

20

terms to her cavalier attitude toward men.'

'I guess it's an old story in your experience, Judge,' Edge offered to fill another pause that seemed to be left purposefully by Benedict.

The man aboard the buggy vented a sound of avid agreement. 'I should say so, sir. In my experience, there are as many crimes of violence perpetrated because of the relationships between men and women as there are on account of greed for money.'

Then he cleared his throat and his tone became earnest, in the manner of a man nearing a point he would rather not discuss but knowing it cannot be avoided. 'John Grady—Curly as he was known by almost everyone in Winton—claimed to have found the corpse by accident. In a ditch on a vacant lot immediately across Travis Street from the theatre. Ran hell for leather to the sheriff's office, shouting his head off about what he had found.'

His attitude not at all like that of an experienced judge, the old man in the buggy once more grasped an opportunity to deviate from the subject. 'I will not cite names, Mr Edge, and it doesn't apply only to the towns on my present circuit up here in Oregon. But many of the peace officers I have had dealings with leave much to be desired in how they carry out their duties.

'But not so Sheriff Kenyon in Winton, sir. He is a credit to his profession. I have never had call to question any evidence he has produced in the past: and neither did I during the trial of John Grady for the rape and murder of Miss Teresa Ward. And against this, there was not a shred of evidence that could be construed as providing reasonable doubt in favour of the boy.'

He shook his head, uttered a sound of regret. 'Just the boy himself—he would have been eighteen years old on the day after he was hanged—Fletcher Grady, his father, and a woman of somewhat questionable morals maintained Curly could not have committed the crime. But the two accounts did not tally. The boy's father and his friend stated he was with them. Which was unlikely in view of the kind of relationship between Grady senior and Miss Roxanne

Graham. While the boy later told Nicholas—Sheriff Kenyon—he was walking in the hills, plunged several times into the Clearwater Swimming Hole east of town while he tried to overcome his feelings for Miss Ward who was to leave Winton the following morning.'

'How you tell it, Judge, I can see how it seemed to be such an open and shut case,' Edge said, found he had gotten increasingly intrigued by the business which he had been drawn into the fringe of at dawn. As the white-whiskered old-timer talked about it in such a convoluted way.

'Quite, sir. And Sheriff Kenyon suspected it would be from shortly after the terrified young man reported the murder. Not only because the boy was frightened out of his wits. Most people would be terribly upset to make such a grisly discovery. But Nicholas Kenyon knew from personal experience that Curly was one of those most smitten by the undeniable charms of Miss Ward. Who had been heard in public to taunt him for his youthful awkwardness. Humiliated him, you understand?'

'Even from this distance,' Edge said, 'the kid is looking like he did it sure enough.'

'Quite. But nevertheless the sheriff carried out his duty to the full. He talked to countless local men who had made it known, mostly with loose talk in the Oregon Trail Saloon, that they admired Miss Ward. And he made enemies of some of them by his insistence in questioning them. For certain wives got to hear about it and this led to domestic strife.'

He paused, frowned like he was recalling some domestic strife of his own. Then shrugged off the memory, returned to the subject of the rape and murder of Teresa Ward. 'It became clearer and clearer to the sheriff that only young Grady could not reasonably account for his whereabouts at the time of the poor girl's ordeal and murder. For he did not believe the highly suspect story that Curly was with his father and his father's ... lady friend.'

Edge asked evenly: 'Roxanne Graham the local whore, Judge?'

'What ...? Goodness gracious, no!' Benedict was spluttering. 'The town council and Nicholas Kenyon would never countenance a woman of that kind in Winton, sir! No, Mrs Graham is a widow woman who... Well, sir, we are both travelling men of the world, I would say?'

'The world of a lot of the United States and a little of Mexico in my case, Judge.'

'Yes, quite. My own travels have been confined by the borders of my native land. But we both know what I mean. We know women have much the same needs as men. And widows, after an appropriate period of mourning, seem often in my experience to have more pressing needs than other husbandless women who... Well again, I'm certain you get my drift, sir?'

It was plain to Edge that Charles C. Benedict was something of a womaniser: his apparent shock a mere pretence.

'Your friend at the farm south of the trail a widow woman, Judge?'

'What's that? Sir, I resent the implications you make and——'

'No sweat, Judge,' Edge broke in evenly as they reached the crest of a hill beyond which a broad plateau spread, less densely cloaked with timber. Up here in the higher ground, the sky began to brighten as the slate-grey clouds thinned, even showed streaks of white here and there. The smell of rain-sodden ground was less dank and the air felt a little warmer. The sun stayed in solid cover. 'I thought we were men of the world, so I——'

'All right!' Benedict broke back in stiffly, sniffed as he felt the need to explain: 'The Widow Hussy was married to the best friend I made in the profession, sir. An attorney in Portland. Miriam invested the money Raymond left her in a poultry farm. I call upon her whenever I can to see she is still all right.'

'Sure, Judge.'

'Not that it is any of your business, sir.'

'None of this is,' Edge pointed out evenly. 'But you need to talk and I've got no reason not to listen.'

'Yes.' He nodded. 'Good.'

'Which Mrs Graham isn't.'

'What?'

'Roxanne Graham isn't a whore, but she's not a good woman, Judge.'

Benedict vented a sound that could have conveyed his disapproval of either Edge or the Widow Graham, said: 'She is a lady who could be much more discreet in pursuit of fulfilling her needs, Mr Edge. She does not sell her favours for money: which would not be allowed in a town such as Winton. Not that Mrs Graham has any financial worries. The bakery she has run since the death of her husband is highly profitable. But . . . let me just say that Fletcher Grady is not the first man to enjoy her hospitality. And I doubt very much he'll be the last.'

Fleetingly, after a glance into the interior of the buggy when he saw the rancorous anger on the judge's face, Edge wondered if the old man had been a former recipient of the Widow Graham's favours: or if he had tried and been rejected. But then the bewhiskered man met the impassive gaze of the narrowed blue eyes, glared a tacit warning that the subject of the woman's loose morals was closed. Then:

'To return to the point, sir. The Grady father and son and Mrs Graham adhered to their story throughout Sheriff Kenyon's investigation. But in the end the boy was arrested. Just two days before I was due to hear cases at the Winton Court House.

'I am not one to trumpet my own qualities, sir. I think if you were to speak to anyone who knows me either personally or professionally, they would bear me out. It is a matter of common consent that I endeavour at all times to be as much of a credit to my calling as, let us say, Nicholas Kenyon is to his.'

'I believe you, Judge,' Edge said as he took out the makings of a cigarette.

'Am I making too much of my integrity, sir? Perhaps I am. But I want you to be assured that the trial of John Grady was as fair as any I have presided over. Perhaps a lot fairer than most even. Since Sheriff Kenyon is so honest. And it was firmly established that the twelve jury members were all unbiased.'

He sighed, shook his head, dropped the pitch of his voice. 'It was of short duration: lasted less than an hour. The boy abruptly broke down under my questioning. Admitted he was not with his father and Mrs Graham. Substituted an account of his movements that could not be corroborated, even by another's perjury.

'After this, the jury did not even withdraw to deliberate on a verdict. The foreman called for a show of hands and there was a unanimous guilty vote without a moment's hesitation.

'John Grady was taken the next day to Klamath and within a week he was hanged, his remains buried in the prison grounds.'

'About three months ago,' Edge said on a stream of cigarette smoke as he flicked away the dead match.

'Yes.' Benedict sounded exhausted from so much talk, the disturbing memories the events of the morning had resurrected.

'Now somebody figures you all got it wrong.'

Charles C. Benedict made a sound like he was going to take issue with this bald statement. Then, his voice thick with something akin to anguish, he agreed: 'Quite. And it is plain who that person is. Although young Curly Grady was well known locally, I gathered he was not particularly well liked. He was something of a loner who preferred to keep his own company. In a close-knit community, that does not engender affection.

'I cannot imagine that anyone but his father would go to the trouble of staging that grisly scene back there. Fletcher Grady was quite understandably embittered by the outcome of the trial. It was only natural he would be. I am accustomed to receiving vindictive abuse from the family and friends of guilty men. But invariably time has a calming effect on them.'

'Unless somebody can prove a mistake was made, Judge?'

'Yes, quite. But if new evidence has come to light in this case, I'm sure I would have heard of it. Unofficially by telegraph or a letter from Nicholas Kenyon, who I consider a friend as well as a colleague in the business of maintaining law and order. And officially through the channels that are open to keep me informed of what I need to know while I'm engaged on circuit work.'

'Unless it only just came to light, Judge. Winton people would know you'd be coming into town on this trail today?'

'Yes. Yes, of course. It's essential my calendar is known in advance so that courtrooms and cases for trial can be prepared. Yes, I suppose something could have been discovered coincidentally with my duty visit to Winton. Though I'm inclined to think that gruesome exhibit back on the trail was the work of a demented mind. And if that is so, the poor man is to be pitied rather than punished.'

'But, Judge?'

'What?'

'It sounded like you weren't going to leave it at that?'

'Yes. yes. Quite so. I'll overlook this one incident if Fletcher Grady agrees not to indulge in such grisly pranks again. But if he attempts to frighten me or anyone else connected with the case in the future, then action will have to be taken. Would you not agree, sir?'

Edge replied evenly: 'Don't ask me, feller. I've never claimed to be the best judge of anything.'

3

Winton was a prosperous community in a valley of the Cascade Mountain foothills through which the Beaver River ran, north to south.

It was an old established town with two broad thoroughfares that vied for being regarded as the main one. Travis Street was a mile-long stretch of the trail that ran parallel with the river. Juniper was a half-mile-long section of the east to west trail, intersecting Travis and bridging the Beaver at the centre of town.

The richly-soiled valley had been settled early by easterners off the wagon trains who had no desire to see what lay on the other side of the Cascade Range.

Most of the older buildings—false fronted stores to supply the needs of the farm people scattered along the valley and the single-story houses in which the storekeepers and their families lived—were of timber. But as the town developed and spread, brick and stone were extensively used for premises that rose to two and even three stories.

It was a fine, proud town peopled by decent, upright citizens who had little call for a courthouse. The murder of Teresa Ward was the first serious crime to happen in Winton since a series of arson attacks committed by a wronged wife fifteen years earlier. But the courthouse was one of the most elaborate of any the judge had ever presided in outside of cities.

Winton was that kind of town, possessed of a great deal of civic pride: the people took as much care over maintaining their public buildings as their houses and business premises.

Edge learned these unasked for geographical and historical facts about the town in the Beaver River Valley from Judge Charles C. Benedict as they completed the trip. From their

27

meeting place, at what he called Timber Bluff, to a point where the trail dipped over the eastern crest of the north-south valley and they could see the community at a distance of perhaps three miles.

Winton, for which the judge obviously had a high regard, was just one subject he covered during the talking jag that kept him from worrying about what awaited him there this grey, damp, chill, late-winter morning.

At the start, no matter what aspect of his life and work the judge spoke of, Edge interjected the occasional query or short response to show he was listening: albeit without much interest most of the time. But it soon became clear the man no longer needed this kind of encouragement: so long as he could talk and had a listener to give his talk a purpose of sorts.

Sometimes he veered toward disjointed rambling and his voice got to be barely audible. Occasionally he talked himself dry. Or into a corner where he lost the thread of what he was saying. Which irritated him, or made him morose as his mind began to dwell on the matter he most wanted to forget. Whenever this happened, he seemed even older than he was; on the verge of senility and not in the least like a man experienced in reaching considered judgments that could mean the difference between living and dying for those who stood before him.

He did not begin to provide information about the town of Winton until they were drawing close to it: and only as they reached the top of the rise and could look down into the Beaver River Valley did he make reference to the Teresa Ward killing. Spoke in a nervous tone that conveyed his mounting concern about the possible repercussions of the trial that were waiting for him.

Then, as they started to ride and drive along the looping curves of the trail down into the valley, the judge said with heartfelt relief:

'Well, it looks much as usual, Mr Edge.'

The half-breed confined his response to an affirmative monosyllable: could have pointed out that nothing short of a disastrous fire or an earthquake would have made Winton

28

look any different over the distance at which they saw it.

As Edge put names to the two broad thoroughfares that intersected in the middle of town, he acknowledged that Benedict had painted an accurate picture of Winton. There had been no need to mention the several narrower streets that ran off both sides of Travis and Juniper. Nor had the judge mentioned there was a poor section in this proud community: a rundown area of timber and tin shacks sprawled along both banks of the Beaver River in the north west quarter of town.

As he made this cursory survey of Winton, Edge found himself voluntarily thinking along a line suggested by Benedict's final comment. And he contemplated moving off the trail at any of many convenient points, to swing around the south eastern side of town. To get on to the south trail that, after it started at the end of Travis Street, with the river curved out of sight down the valley.

But he did not give serious thought to the notion: called himself a fool for considering it at all. For he needed trail supplies, his horse could use two new shoes. And some hot, home-cooked food, a couple of beers, maybe a shot or two of rye would not go amiss. Nor would a night in a comfortable bed under a sound roof.

It was crazy to contemplate detouring past the town where all this was available just because of a three-month-old murder trial that was none of his concern.

The closer they got to the eastern fringe of Winton, Benedict remaining tensely silent—almost like he was afraid to speak because he was worried it might be tempting providence—the more normal the town looked. And the clearer it became to Edge that this was indeed a mostly prosperous community filled with ordinary people going about their everyday business.

The noosed rope suspended from the oak tree branch seemed very far removed from here: much more than ten miles and two hours in distance and time.

It was not even out of the ordinary, in Edge's experience, to have the local sheriff ride out from a town to meet him. Although it was not usual for the lawman to raise an arm in welcome.

Benedict revealed it was the local peace officer who rode off the end of Juniper Street before they were close enough to see such a detail as the badge pinned to the left lapel of his suit jacket.

'That'll be Nicholas, I guess,' the judge said with near breathless relief in his voice as he craned forward in the buggy to peer down the final slope of the trail. 'Sheriff Kenyon. Always makes a point of coming out to meet me. My eyes aren't what they used to be, Mr Edge. Does he look at his ease?'

'I can't see that either, Judge,' the half-breed replied. 'Can tell you he doesn't have a hand near the gun in his holster.'

Benedict was easy enough in his own mind to welcome another topic of conversation. He said pensively: 'I guess that's how lawman new to you usually act when they see you riding into their town, uh?'

Edge showed a quiet, cold-eyed grin as he answered: 'I've had more than my fair share of trouble with lawmen, Judge.'

'That does not surprise me, sir,' Benedict said, a little ruefully. 'In my line of business I endeavour not to prejudge anything on first impression. Especially my fellow human beings. But I have to admit, at first sight your demeanour does call to mind many of the kind of men I've seen as prisoners in my courts. Which is not to say, of course ... Well, I can understand how small town sheriffs might be——'

'I am what I am, Judge,' Edge put in to get the old man out of this latest corner he had talked himself into.

Benedict sighed, nodded. 'We all are, sir. And many are not as they seem. Tell me, are we close enough yet to see if the sheriff is smiling?'

Edge returned his attention to the man riding the piebald horse just as Kenyon reined the animal to a halt alongside the town limits marker. Which was newly painted, black on white, and possible to read over a distance of several hundred feet: WINTON THE PROUDEST TOWN IN OREGON.

It could also be seen that the lawman's expression either altered into a frown, or deepened into a more pronounced look of perturbation.

'He's not happy man, Judge,' Edge supplied. 'But that

could be on account of him getting a first impression of me.'

'Oh, dear,' Benedict muttered grimly, gave a quick shake of his head. 'No, sir. Nicholas is just like me in that respect. He tries not to let the looks of a man influence his opinion. And so I fear——'

'Charles!' Kenyon called. 'I sure am glad to see you made it safe to town. Howdy, stranger.'

'It's good to be back, Nicholas!' the judge responded over the final two hundred feet of trail to the start of Juniper Street. Then he lowered his voice, said out of the side of his prominent mouth: 'I don't like the sound of that, Mr Edge. About me making it safely to town.'

If it required any effort for the sheriff to put a false face on his true feelings, it had been made by the time Edge and Benedict reached him. And he wheeled his horse so he could ride back into town on the other side of the buggy from Edge. He wasn't smiling, but neither did he frown. He eyed Edge with frank curiosity but, just as Benedict had predicted, he did not seem to have come to any instant conclusions about the impassive half-breed.

'What did you mean by——' Benedict started to ask anxiously.

'You're a stranger to these parts, aren't you, mister?' Kenyon put in quickly, eager to block the line of talk the judge tried to open.

'Right, Sheriff.'

'This is Mr Edge, Nicholas,' Benedict introduced hurriedly. 'Mr Edge, Sheriff Nicholas Kenyon, good friend and highly regarded colleague. Edge and I met out at Timber Bluff, Nicholas. Where the damndest thing happened——'

'You plan to stay in Winton, Mr Edge?' Kenyon interrupted.

'Awhile maybe. Heading for California.'

'You couldn't find a better town to rest up in, mister,' the lawman said. Was able to use enthusiasm as a ploy to ignore the judge.

But just for a moment when he met the half-breed's narrow eyed gaze across the back of the gelding in the buggy's traces, he expressed a less amiable feeling. Whether deliberately or not, hinted perhaps that if Charles C. Benedict was not riding between them in the cut-under rig, he would have a much different attitude toward the travel-stained, unshaven, dishevelled, rifle-and-revolver-toting stranger.

Then the lawman faced front, launched into a catalogue of the amenities his town provided for transient visitors.

He was a match for Edge's age. Was an inch or so shorter and several pounds heavier: much of the excess weight sagging around his middle and across his chest. The dark blue suit he wore revealed he had been putting on the extra pounds recently: for it was relatively new but decidedly close fitting. It was not just the gunbelt slung around his bulging waist that prevented him fastening the jacket.

He had a handsome face, the skin burnished an even light brown. Crinkles rather than wrinkles were spread at the sides of his clear, dark eyes and broad, finely-shaped mouth. It was the kind of face which, if he did not have a thin moustache—blonder than his eyebrows and the hair and sideburns that showed beneath the brim of his grey Stetson—and a slightly crooked nose, would have lacked character. Instead, it was the face of a man who looked like he could switch from easy friendliness to vicious meanness in an instant: show his change of feeling by the slightest alteration to the mouthline, the level of light in his eyes.

He demonstrated this as he glanced back into the buggy when Benedict said insistently:

'I was about to ask what you meant about me arriving safely, Nicholas. Why shouldn't I?'

'Just a figure of speech, Charles,' the suddenly smiling lawman said evenly. Then he directed another pointed glance at Edge: his broad mouth still smiling, but his dark eyes not, as he told the half-breed in the same tone: 'Now don't you forget, mister. Bill and Kath's Winton Hotel is the best place to stay in town. And you be sure to tell them I said to give you extra special treatment.'

He laughed, but it had the hollow ring of false good humour. 'Won't get you a red cent off the tab, but maybe it'll make Bill Henderson smile a little more than he usually does. On account of he took better than ten bucks off me playing poker last night and he'll surely enjoy recollecting that.'

'Much obliged.'

'Way you get there, you ride on down Juniper to the crossing at Travis, swing left and it's just along on the west side of the street. Two floors high, stone built: you can't miss it.'

'I'd like to head straight for the hotel myself, Nicholas,' the judge said wearily. 'Could use a hot bath, get the damp out of my old bones, before I——'

'Be best if you stop by the office, Charles,' the lawman cut in. Made no secret now he was concerned over something the presence of Edge kept him from raising. 'There's some law business I need to discuss with you before court sits this afternoon.'

Benedict said earnestly: 'If it's what I think it is, Nicholas, Mr Edge is already familiar with the matter, so——'

'As familiar as I want to get, Judge,' Edge said, gazed levelly at Kenyon and failed to see relief or any kind of gratitude for his co-operative attitude. Instead, the lawman expressed narrow-eyed suspicion about Edge's involvement with Benedict: irrespective of whether it had anything to do with the worry that concerned him.

Then the half-breed looked back at the nervous, old man in the buggy, starting now to get angry, and drawled: 'If I don't run into you again, Judge, luck to you.'

'And to you, Mr Edge,' Benedict answered, his demeanour mellowing. 'I've appreciated your company on the trail, sir.'

'Like I told you, I was riding this way,' the half-breed said with a shrug.

Benedict was not concerned by the cynicism of Edge's reply, pointed out: 'But you didn't have to hold back. Subject yourself to the pace and the ramblings of an old man.'

They had covered half the length of the busy with people Juniper Street between the limits marker and the mid-town intersection: moving between well maintained houses in back of neatly fenced front yards on the south side, stores with well filled display windows to the north.

Beyond a line of stores with a shared sidewalk crowded with morning shoppers and intent gossipers was the recently

33

repainted, red brick law office. It had a net-curtained window at each side of a glass panelled door with Kenyon's name and title on it in gold blocked black lettering. If there were cells in the building, they were at the rear.

The lawman angled his horse toward the alley-flanked building, indicated with an emphatic jerk of his head the judge should steer the buggy in the same direction. A grimace showed he was ready to get mad at either his old friend or the stranger if his wishes were not met.

Benedict complied with a sigh, then called after Edge, who kept riding a straight line along the street: 'Don't break any laws, Mr Edge!'

The half-breed turned in the saddle to reply in the same light tone used by the old man: 'Don't want to court trouble, so I'll try not to, Judge.'

Benedict laughed and it sounded only slightly of being forced.

Kenyon snarled as he swung down from his saddle out front of the law office: 'While you're in my jurisdiction, you better do more than try, mister!'

Benedict vented an impatient grunt, suddenly sounded very weary as he explained: 'It was a joke, Nicholas. Court...? Try...? Judge...?'

Kenyon shook his head irritably, then said ominously to the old man: 'What I have to tell you is no laughing matter, Charles.'

Edge growled as he snapped a forefinger against the front underside of his hat brim: 'Got you, Sheriff. No funny business.'

4

That cold but clear evening the elaborately carved, highly polished grandfather clock in the elegantly furnished lobby of the Winton Hotel had struck the final note to mark the hour of seven when the gunshot was triggered.

Edge momentarily paused as he lifted a spoonful of fish soup from a bowl toward his mouth when Kath Henderson squealed:

'Goodness, was that what I thought it was?'

He told the woman, who had frozen in process of setting the next table to his, 'Ma'am, if you thought it was a handgun being fired, you're right.'

Mrs Henderson, a tall and thin, once fine looking and now rather haggard woman of fifty or so, stared at Edge for stretched seconds: either had not understood what he said, failed to comprehend his unruffled attitude, or was still in a state of shock.

Then she snapped out of the petrified stance, shook her head, gasped, whirled and went out of the dining room at a run: her gait ungainly because her black and white dress had not been designed for that kind of frenetic movement by its wearer.

Just before the door crashed into its frame behind her, Bill Henderson yelled frantically: 'Kath! Kath, come quick! There's been an accident.'

And this revelation signalled a chorus of voices, calling and answering at once, so the result was a cacophony out of which Edge heard nothing that made any sense. But he did not, anyway, attempt to pick out anything coherent from the babble of voices as he continued unhurriedly to spoon up the good-tasting soup from the bowl. Relishing this as another welcome luxury of the Winton Hotel that so far had lived up to everything Judge Benedict and Sheriff Kenyon had claimed for it.

So had as much of the town as he had seen of it since he had left the two men out front of the law office and ridden to the hotel. Where, right off, the liveryman who had premises immediately next door to the two-story stone hotel building emerged from his stable and offered to take the roan gelding to the blacksmith for two new shoes before seeing to it the animal was fed, watered and sheltered for as long as necessary.

When Edge entered the hotel lobby, the Henderson husband and wife eyed him, his saddle and bedroll, with something less than enthusiasm for such a guest. Until he mentioned he had been travelling with Benedict and that the judge and local sheriff had both recommended him to stay at this hotel.

This spread a warm smile across the face of the woman, her husband to make a sound that might have been of pleasure. He was as thin as his wife, but whereas her sparsely-fleshed features had a basically kindly form to them, his face was inscribed with countless lines that all had a downward curve at their ends. Which gave his countenance the mournful look that had led to his reputation for being a less than happy individual.

But something close to a toothy smile parted his lips and turned up their corners when Edge drew a healthy roll of bills from a hip pocket, asked how much he needed to pay in advance for a night's stay with meals. And after he requested a hot bath to get rid of the trail dirt of long travel he was made to feel as welcome as any neat and clean, dudishly attired guest who had arrived on the stage.

The rooms were as well furnished as the carpeted lobby and balustraded stairway promised. Then, after a bath and shave, he dusted off his clothing and went down to eat a midday meal: felt contented enough, the food was good enough, so that he was able to suppress the impulse to irritation he otherwise might have felt at being an object of curiosity.

He had sat by choice at a table in a bay window of the wood-panelled dining room, as he ate was aware of surreptitious glances directed in at him from passers-by on the street as well as from his fellow guests. For most of the time he sensed only the idle curiosity of people for a stranger in their midst. But every now and then he detected a deeper interest than this in the eyes that looked at him, then quickly away to avoid meeting his cool gaze.

He thought that some of his fellow guests came close to approaching him with pointed queries that would have revealed precisely why his arrival in Winton had been talked about. But none of them communicated with him at all outside of a nod or a briefly spoken greeting, a reference to the dull weather.

Kath Henderson, who waited at table, and her husband, who was the chef, asked only if he was comfortable, had everything he needed.

It was as he left the dining room that he glimpsed Judge Benedict, the bewhiskered old-timer leaving the hotel in a hurry. Mrs Henderson saw the half-breed looking after the quickly-moving figure, explained:

'Court's being held this afternoon, of course. The sheriff kept the poor man talking so long he only had time for a quick bite in his room before rushing out.'

Because he had spent a couple of hours with Benedict, knew something of the old-timers' anxieties, Edge found himself harbouring a degree of sympathy for him as he watched the man scuttle diagonally across the street. Heading for the lion-flanked entrance of the impressive, granite-built courthouse. And Edge gained a strong impression that whatever had been said in the law office came as bad news. For Charles C. Benedict this afternoon looked both exhausted and utterly dejected; even less fitted to apply himself to the solemn business of judging his fellow men.

But once Benedict was out of sight, he was out of mind. And Edge left the hotel to shop for supplies: discovered people reacted to him much as when he was in the hotel dining room. More people were interested in him than were not. But nobody seemed to be afraid of him, as could sometimes happen when he appeared in a strange town: one of the few men—sometimes, as in this case, the only one—on the street to carry a gun in a tied-down holster.

Winton people were discreetly, mostly politely curious about him. And storekeepers and fellow customers either masked their interest with friendly greetings or quickly looked away whenever he met their quizzical gazes.

Edge did not enjoy the shopping chore at the best of times. And it got to be increasingly difficult to keep his irritation with the people around him under control.

So he felt a sense of weary relief when he stepped back into his quiet room on the second floor at the front of the hotel, stripped down to his longjohns and stretched out under the crisply clean covers on the comfortable bed.

He immediately fell into the sleep of the contented. But came awake in the dusk-darkened room with a disconcerting start: his first conscious thoughts concerned with being inescapably trapped by burdensome responsibilities in a town like Winton Oregon. Where it was probably against a local ordinance to spit in the street, if a man did not wear a clean shirt every day he was considered a low dirty bum and women—except for Roxanne Graham—allowed you to maybe kiss their hands after six weeks of concentrated courting.

Just the kind of quiet, clean, decent community that would hold an appeal for a one-time rich Virginian dude like Adam Steele!

These first waking notions triggered by the new life-style he had heard Steele had adopted soured Edge's mind with a degree of ill humour worse than that caused by the inquisitiveness of Winton people this afternoon. The feeling stayed with him until, as he got dressed, he smelled the aroma of cooking meat wafted up from the hotel kitchen.

This as full night came to the Beaver River Valley and the darkness beyond the window of the room began to be pricked with bright gleams of yellow lamp light.

It did not look like there would be any rain tonight, which was good. Since later he intended to take a stroll along the

38

western stretch of Juniper Street. To where, this afternoon, he had spotted the sign out front of the Oregon Trail Saloon on the other side of the river bridge.

He was the first guest for supper and told Mrs Henderson he would wait, kill the time with the latest edition of the *Winton Examiner* he had gotten from a pile on a table in the lobby. But she assured him eagerly it was no trouble to serve him right way: and only briefly did he consider this eagerness might be because she would prefer him to be through when the rest of the hotel's guests showed up to eat.

He felt a flare of anger at this notion which came to him unbidden. Was aware of the scowl that spread involuntarily across his face as he linked this disturbing sense of inferiority to the comparisons he kept making between himself and Steele.

But he was impassive again before Mrs Henderson returned with the fish soup he had ordered as a starter to a T-bone steak. Barred unwelcome lines of thought from his mind as he began to enjoy the soup while the woman worked at setting the next table, the clock in the lobby struck seven times and the gunshot exploded upstairs.

Before he finished the soup the level of sound outside the tranquil peace of the softly lit dining room had subsided to a distant hushed whispering, interspersed from time to time with expectant pauses.

He had set down his spoon in the empty bowl, was reaching for the folded newspaper on the other side of the table when the door opened. And a pretty redhead with large eyes and full lips peered in. Her eyes grew larger, her mouth dropped open and after what seemed like a long time she gasped in a shocked tone:

'Oh, it's you and you're here?'

'Right,' Edge told her flatly, recalled seeing her in one of the stores this afternoon. Now realised why she had seemed vaguely familiar to him then. For against the backdrop of the Winton Hotel he could recognise she was a younger, fuller bodied version of Kath Henderson with the hair colour of Bill Henderson. 'Here I am, and I ain't nobody else.'

'But I thought you'd have... That you'd be——'

'Where did it happen, Miss Mary?' Nicholas Kenyon demanded harshly from out in the lobby as the entrance doors banged behind him.

The woman opened the door wide as she turned toward the lawman, who glimpsed Edge at the table and came to a sudden halt: glowered acrimoniously at the half-breed. Then tore his gaze away from the impassive eyes when the woman answered:

'In his room, Sheriff. Number ten on the second floor.'

The sheriff, his lips as tight as his suit, lunged forward and started heavy footed up the staircase as Mary Henderson returned her censuring gaze to Edge, said:

'I'd have thought you'd want to go take a look.'

'What at, ma'am?'

'Why, the . . . Oh, my goodness!' She pressed a hand to her mouth, blinked her large eyes. 'You don't know who it is has been shot?'

'That's right.'

'The Judge! Judge Benedict, Mr Edge! He was shot through the back of the head! Like some dog had to be put down!'

His first impulse was to rise slowly from the chair, leave the dining room and go up the stairs in the wake of the lawman. But the anger remained confined in an ice cold ball at the pit of his stomach. And within a matter of moments the instinct to involve himself was gone. He began to think of Judge Charles C. Benedict as just a nice old-timer he had spent a little trail riding time with. Now he had been shot dead: and the feller whose job it was to take care of such events in this town was already doing what needed to be done. He said, aware that his tone of voice was taut:

'That's a damn shame, ma'am.'

'A shame?' she rasped bitterly, something akin to contempt on her pale face which now had splashes of crimson at the centre of the cheeks. 'Is that all you can say?'

Edge sighed, growled: 'It's all I have to say about the judge being dead, Miss Henderson. On another subject I'd like to say the soup was fine and I'll be happy to have the steak whenever it's convenient.'

For a stretched second she was on the point of blurting a caustic retort at Edge. But then she caught her breath, did a double-take at him, shook her head and showed undisguised contempt when she accused: 'Oh, of course! You're one of those hard men of the frontier we hear about, uh? Afraid to show your feelings because you think that makes you seem soft?'

'Like I told somebody else earlier today, Miss Henderson,' he replied evenly. 'I am what I am.'

'I'm impressed at how tough you are!' she sneered around the mounting rage that constricted her throat. 'We don't get many of your kind staying at this hotel.'

'Seems to me you should have a lot of us, Miss Henderson.'

'Just why should you think that?' She was unable to see through his veneer of dispassion and recognise the anger the exchange was stirring within him. Felt no need to disguise her own feelings toward him.

'With the service being so slow, should be a lot of hungry people.'

Her grimacing glower became more firmly set as she snapped: 'A man has just been shot dead in the hotel!'

He nodded. 'Guess that makes a change.'

'I'll say it does make a change! This is the first——'

'Usually the guests die from hunger?'

5

Mary Henderson slammed the door with deliberate force, using the gesture as an outlet for her emotions which words could not express. It made a much louder crash than when her mother left the dining room and Edge winced as he reached across the table for the newspaper.

He ignored the first page, which was filled with advertisements for stores, services, property and the next meetings of various organisations in Winton and the surrounding area of the Beaver River Valley. He did not expect to find much of any greater interest to a passing-through stranger on the other three pages of the *Winton Examiner*.

But he was wrong.

The main story which took up the first two columns on the second page of the broadsheet newspaper was considered important enough to be headlined in type twice as large as any other. So it would have caught his attention even if he had not gotten involved on the fringes of the events it covered:

TRAGEDY OF JOHN GRADY
THESPIAN CONFESSES THEN
KILLS HIMSELF

The account was as leadenly written as were most contributions to western newspapers. Needed to be combed through from the first to the last line for all the salient fresh facts to be extracted.

In this instance there was a re-telling of the rape and murder of Teresa Ward, then a reiteration of Grady's arrest and trial. Three months ago.

Two days ago, Sheriff Nicholas Kenyon had received a

telegraph from San Francisco, sent by the city's Chief of Police. The message stated that an actor named Theodore Brigden had shot himself through the head in a dressing room of a Market Street theatre. He had left a note confessing the suicide was an act of remorse for murdering Teresa Ward in Winton Oregon. He had strangled her in a fit of uncontrolled rage caused by his insane jealousy. His burden of anguish was even harder to bear because he had allowed another man to go to the gallows for his crime.

Edge had just finished reading the editorial comment on the news from San Francisco—in which the *Examiner*'s editor sought to placate the guilt feelings sure to be experienced by those directly involved with the miscarriage of justice—when the dining room door opened again. And Sheriff Nicholas Kenyon stepped through, closed the door softly behind him. He looked sick to his stomach, and seemed afraid to speak for several seconds.

Until the half-breed prompted: 'Something I can do for you, Sheriff?'

'I see you've just read the paper?' he answered thickly and leaned his back against the door. One hand was behind him, like he was grasping the knob to guard doubly against anybody entering.

Edge folded the newspaper, nodded.

'The account of the actor—Brigden—confessing to the Ward murder? Then putting a bullet in his brain? Down in San Francisco?'

'Right, Sheriff. I just read about all that.'

Kenyon grimaced and brought his hidden hand into sight. It was clenched into a tight first around a length of rope fashioned into a noose. He held it aloft as he said grimly: 'The judge told me about the rope tied to the tree out at Timber Bluff this morning. And the sign nailed to the tree. Said he told you about the case we had against young Grady.'

'That's what he did, Sheriff.'

'Charles is dead now. Shot in the back of the head. This thing was fixed to the front of his shirt with a pin.'

Kenyon moved his hand holding the noose, eyed it gingerly like it was something with a malevolent life of its own that

43

could harm him. Then looked expectantly at the half-breed.

Edge said: 'Benedict figured it was a warning meant for him, Sheriff.'

'I know. He was pretty badly shaken up by it even before I told him what you've just been reading in the *Examiner*. Told him how I heard from Frisco about that actor killing himself and leaving the note. How I felt duty-bound to tell Fletcher Grady. How the whole town would know about it after the O'Hara brothers printed it in the newspaper today. I had to make it public.'

The lawman seemed to be drawing further and further back into a state of morose detachment. Was like a man going through the motions of doing his duty, no part of his heart in it.

'It's the kind of news always gets spread, one way or another,' Edge said, in no hurry to have Kenyon get to the point.

'Charles and me agreed on that. When I decided to let local folks know, I thought there'd just be some bad mouthing from the kind of folks who are always wise after the event.'

Now he became even more withdrawn. Stared into the middle distance, his lips beneath the moustache moving almost imperceptibly: like he was seeing a parade of these people. Was counting them off, or maybe naming them.

Edge asked: 'You know who killed him, Sheriff?'

'What?' He was jerked back into the here and now by the simply-stated question. Was suddenly rattled as he bunched up the truncated hanging rope, shoved it into a side pocket of his too-tight suit jacket. Demanded: 'How the hell can I know that for sure? I was damn sure I knew who killed the Ward girl!'

Edge shrugged. 'I've got time to kill waiting for my steak. Way you're using time telling me what I already know, it seems like you've got this thing——'

'I've got good reason to be here, mister!' He held off from giving the reason, head cocked in a listening attitude.

Beyond the confines of the dining room, the hotel and the street immediately outside had been quiet for some time. Now a wagon was heard to halt out front, the hotel entrance doors opened, questions were asked by a man, answers given by a woman and footfalls creaked on the stairway.

And while the half-breed and the sheriff listened to this, Kenyon brought his impulse to anger under firm control. But continued to fill time with inconsequentials: putting off the inevitable.

'That'll be Frank Behan's men, come to pick up the body,' he said dully. 'Behan's the undertaker for the valley.'

'You want to go and check they do things right, feel free,' Edge invited, starting to tire of the lawman's stalling.

And the hint of acid in his tone got to Kenyon.

'What were you saying? Oh, yeah: I'm hoping this won't turn out to be a waste of time, Edge. Talking with you.' It had started out hard toned. But then he sounded unsure of himself again. 'It's obvious I've got an idea about who killed Charles. But it just doesn't seem the style of the man to take all that trouble with setting up the warning out at Timber Bluff.' He touched his fingertips to a jacket pocket. 'Leave this string the way it was left on the body.'

The doorknob rattled and he stepped quickly away from the door, pulled it open. And Kath Henderson came in, with a tray on which Edge's supper plate gave off aromatic steam.

'Oh!' she exclaimed, displaced her disdainful frown with embarrassment as she looked from Edge to Kenyon. 'I'm sorry, I didn't realise you were still in the hotel, Nicholas. This gentleman told Mary he was in a hurry for——'

'That's all right, Kath,' Kenyon assured her indifferently. Then looked with determination at the half-breed, like the presence of a third party had encouraged him to make his point. 'I just have one question for Mr Edge, then he can finish his supper.'

The tall, thin, hollow-eyed, sunken-cheeked woman delivered the supper plate to the table, set it down with a thud that matched her reproachful expression which made the Henderson mother and daughter—as Edge had most recently seen Mary— look very much alike.

'The soup was good, ma'am,' Edge said as she picked up the empty bowl, clattered it on to the tray. 'Steak tastes only half as good as it smells, it'll be the same.'

She replied tautly: 'I only wish I had the kind of constitution would allow me an appetite after such a fine man as Judge Benedict was shot to death under this very roof!'

Edge said evenly: 'Tell you something I wish, ma'am.'

His tone of voice caused her to halt and turn on her way out of the dining room. To look back at him expectantly while the sheriff opened the door for her.

'Yes?'

'There are times when I wish I was more like you, ma'am.'

She waited for him to enlarge on this. When he didn't, instead began to cut into the steak, she plainly considered he was being facetious in some way she did not understand. She made to sweep out of the room, but had to hold back with a startled gasp as two dungaree-clad men moved cautiously across the lobby, carrying a plain pine coffin.

'Tell Frank I'll be over in awhile to see to the paper work,' Kenyon said.

He got a husky monosyllable for a reply, then closed the door as soon as Kath Henderson moved off the threshold. Eyed Edge with much the same degree of disapproval bordering on disgust as had the woman at the way the half-breed had started to eat with undisguised relish. But his voice sounded only slightly strained when he said:

'The judge said you were already at Timber Bluff when he got there this morning?'

'That's right.'

'But I guess you didn't get there in time to see who fixed things up that way with the oak tree?'

'I was there ahead of whoever did it, Sheriff.'

'You what?' He was suddenly in the grip of a degree of excitement that caused him to be more rattled than before.

Edge told him flatly: 'It's not going to help you any, Sheriff.'

'You saw...? Charles didn't tell me that.'

Edge shrugged. 'I didn't tell him. He didn't ask. You did, so I'm telling you. But, like I say, it won't be of——'

'Describe him to me, Edge!' Now there was a sudden demanding earnestness in his voice.

'I can't do that.'

'Either you saw him or you didn't, mister!' Another abrupt change had come over him. There was anger mixed in with nervousness gleaming in his dark eyes. Like he thought he had the killer of the judge dead to rights. And he suspected the half-breed was deliberately concealing vital evidence: facts that would ensure he did not make the same kind of mistake as he did with the last murder in his town.

Edge sighed, chewed a piece of steak and swallowed it before he said: 'I saw him, but I can't tell you it was Fletcher Grady.'

'Damnit, you're a stranger here! I know you don't have any idea what Grady looks like: yet!'

Kenyon needed to struggle to confine his anger to a glower and a tone in his voice. Looked just for a moment like he might lunge into a violent advance from the doorway to the table.

Edge rattled down his fork on the plate, showed his own ice cold anger in how he looked at and spoke to the lawman. 'You want to listen to me tell it, now you've finally gotten around to asking your one question, feller! Or do you want to keep on——'

Kenyon let out a pent up breath through clenched teeth, growled tautly: 'Okay, get it done your way, mister.'

'Obliged, Sheriff. I planned on reaching Winton last night but the rainstorm changed my plans and I bedded down in a hole in the bluff. Around dawn it was still raining and blowing hard, but I heard a horse on the trail, coming from the direction of Winton. I stayed back in the cave because I wasn't in the mood to pass the time of day with anyone who happened to be riding by. But this somebody didn't ride by.'

'So you looked out and saw him?' Kenyon was tensely expectant. He reminded: 'You said you saw him.'

Edge went on evenly: 'After I heard some hammering, which turned out to be of the nails fixing the warning notice for Benedict, I looked out. But I only caught a glimpse of somebody mounting up and starting to ride back the way they came.'

'Some eye witness you are,' Kenyon accused without force. He seemed somehow strangely relieved, like he was now glad

Grady could not be positively identified as the man at the oak.

'I didn't make any claims,' the half-breed countered evenly, shrugged as he picked up his fork again. 'Guess maybe I'd have taken more notice of the rider, or maybe I wouldn't have: but the noosed rope caught my eye for the second or so when there was a gap in the rain. I often pass riders on the trail. Hardly ever see a lynch rope. Especially without somebody's head in the noose.'

'That's what you keep on calling the rider, Edge.'

'What?'

'Somebody.'

'Right.'

'So what you're saying is, it could even have been a woman?'

'From what I saw through the rain, it could have been a trained monkey in a Stetson and slicker, Sheriff.'

Nicholas Kenyon peered hard at Edge, but in a way that indicated this was only because the half-breed happened to be in his line of sight: while he became detached again, his mind filled with images of somebody or something else. Then he grunted, shook his head, growled:

'Can see Roxanne Graham fixing up something like that. But... Shit, I have to figure Grady first.' He gave another grunt, muttered: 'It's a real disappointment, you didn't see enough to recognise who fixed things up that way at the Timber Bluff.'

He had been thinking aloud: even the final remark that had seemed to be addressed to Edge. And when he turned, left the dining room without acknowledging the half-breed, it was like he had forgotten he was not alone.

For ten or fifteen minutes, until the grandfather clock in the lobby struck the hour of eight, Edge was alone. He finished his supper, then read through the rest of the newspaper without paying too much attention to recent Winton happenings which were considered newsworthy enough to get space in its columns.

During this time his mind kept returning to what he said to Kath Henderson: about there being occasions when he wished he could be more like other people in attitudes to violent death. He could not recall ever saying anything like that before. Or even thinking that way. *I am what I am.* That was more his style, so expressed twice today. That other thing... In retrospect he heard the words spoken by somebody else: or at least in a tone of voice he did not recognise as his own.

Other hotel guests began to come down from their rooms for supper. Many were elderly women who all knew each other, so it was clear the place had a resident population of widows and spinsters: all of them comfortably provided for from the jewels that sparkled against expensive fabric or age-cracked flesh. They brought into the dining room an invisible but nearly palpable cloud of cloyingly sweet perfume that almost masked the fragrance of the food they were eating.

A half-dozen city-suited drummers mostly knew each other from this or other stopovers on past sales trips.

Three couples, one pair in their mid-twenties with two young well behaved children, were strangers to each other and everyone else.

The firstcomers chose tables far removed from Edge. Most of his fellow guests pointedly ignored his presence. Some directed disapproval at him and a few of these had the courage of their convictions to meet and hold his quizzical response. But never for more than a second or so after he narrowed his eyes to ice blue glittering slits, expressed a tacit warning to which he let them supply the meaning.

It seemed clear that word of his undemonstrative reaction to the untimely death of the man he rode into town with had been spread and discussed. And those people who had gotten an unflattering first impression of him earlier in the day were now feeling grimly self-satisfied at how they had been right from the start about this unsavoury looking stranger in town.

Talk was slow to begin but as soon as there were enough people in the room for it to be no longer necessary to whisper individual exchanges so as not to be overheard, a hum of conversation built up against the rattling of cutlery and crockery.

The name of Judge Benedict featured often. Likewise those

of Teresa Ward and John Grady. Less so Sheriff Kenyon and Fletcher Grady. The tenor of the gossip varied from shock to regret, indignation to sympathy.

By this time Edge had been rejected as a subject of interest and it felt good to be ignored by the curious and the censorious while his fellow guests talked and ate food served by Kath and Mary Henderson who, he only now noticed, wore identical black and white dresses.

The easy mood stayed with him until he realised he was involuntarily reading the front page of the *Winton Examiner*: his attention concentrated on the listings of properties and businesses for sale. And he uttered an ill-tempered grunt as he folded the paper, slapped it down on the table beside his plate with just the steak bone picked clean on it. Then was startled by a hand that immediately reached down to claim the plate.

Mary Henderson asked: 'Are you thinking of buying a piece of property around here, Mr Edge?'

He looked up, saw no hint of disapproval now: just intrigued interest that matched her tone. And for the first time he registered just how attractive was the pale face in the frame of long auburn hair, with blue eyes of that shade which seems to be green when a redhead has them. Her nose was appealingly uptilted and she had a firm mouthline. But her cheeks were a little bulbous, maybe warned she might be prone to overweight in later years: unless she experienced some of the hard living and worry that had pared down her parents. Right now, though, her black and white dress was attractively filled out by a body that was just a little more heavy than Edge considered his ideal.

Whenever he thought about his ideal woman. Which was not often. But lately he was thinking, saying and doing a great deal that was out of the ordinary for him.

'No, ma'am, I'm not thinking of doing that,' he replied flatly.

'My mistake. I shouldn't have been peeking over your shoulder, should I? Would you like me to bring you a cup of coffee?'

'Much obliged, but I plan a visit to the Oregon Trail for something stronger.'

She answered quickly, with more than a hint of acid: 'You don't need strong drink to calm your shattered nerves, that's plain to see!' Then she immediately softened her expression, like she regretted the impulsive response, offered: 'If you figure to be out after midnight, I'll let you have a key. Midnight's when my parents lock up the hotel. Not many people need a key. There's not much that happens in Winton late at night. Unless there's enough drunks or card-playing fools in the Oregon Trail to make it worthwhile for Jeremiah Harman to stay open.'

She sounded breathless after prattling all this out in an attempt to negate her criticism of him.

Edge told her as he rose from the table: 'I don't have any reason to get drunk and I try not to play cards with fools, Miss Henderson.'

As he turned toward the door, he glimpsed one of the drummers—a dark-eyed man of thirty with slicked down blond hair and a faintly twisted mouth—looking at him with simmering hostility. He failed to understand why this should be, long after everyone else in the room had, albeit reluctantly, accepted his presence as a square peg in the round hole of the Winton Hotel.

At the door, he discovered why the salesman disliked him so much. For as he got his hat from the tree he took a final look around the room, saw the adoring gaze in the eyes of the drummer as he watched Mary Henderson: like he was indelibly registering in his mind every mundane move she made in clearing the dirty dishes off a table shared by three of the bejewelled and expensively-garbed old ladies.

Then, as Mary Henderson turned away from the table, she deliberately or just happened to glance toward the doorway.

Edge tipped his hat to her as he put it on and was surprised by the warmth of her smile. Which triggered a gritted-teeth scowl from the drummer. And next the half-brced was even more surprised at the sexual arousal he felt as he closed the door on the noisy room where, for a moment, the atmosphere had seemed highly charged with silent invitation and a tacit threat of what might happen if the invitation was accepted.

This made Edge feel in even greater need of a drink as he

went out through the double doors and stepped on to the building-wide hotel porch, felt the chill bite of night air on his face.

There was nobody else out on this southern stretch of Travis Street: and glimmers of light from tightly-draped windows and the scent of woodsmoke were evidence that most people had got to wherever they were going tonight. Probably most of them intended to stay there until workaday commitments prised them away from the comfort and warmth in the morning.

He paused at the top of the two steps at the front of the porch, took out the makings and slowly rolled a cigarette. Struck a match on a timber support for the porch roof to light it. Then he looked through the fresh-smelling smoke of the first exhalation mixed in with the mist of his breath in the cold air, peered to his right down to the end of Travis Street: where there was a stone church with a tiled steeple atop its tower on the left, a neatly tended cemetery behind a stone wall opposite.

Beyond this was the dark of the valley that was the first piece of open country he had to ride over to get to where he was going.

Probably for a considerable distance down the valley there were scattered farms and ranches and homesteads where tonight people were as warm and secure and contented as those along Travis and Juniper: the side streets that cut off them. But, somewhere to the south, the unsettled country commenced. The kind of country Edge liked best. Where, without the civilised trappings of town living, or those a man in an isolated house could gather around him, he knew how to stay comfortable and warm on a cold winter night. And contented, too.

No, not anymore, damnit!

If he was still so sure it was the drifting loner's life he liked best, what was he doing here in this crossroads town? Certain of the direction he would take when he rode on out?

All he could be absolutely sure about was that he did not feel at ease with his lot in his present surroundings.

So just where the hell could he be without feeling like a

Goddamn round peg in a lousy square hole? What secret had all these people discovered that he had failed to find no matter where he drifted?

He took the cigarette away from the side of his mouth and spat a stream of saliva into the street. Glimpsed two riders as they emerged out of the darkness beyond the church and cemetery, started northward up Travis Street.

He began to move in the same direction, glanced back once as the two slow-riding men closed the gap on him. Recognised Kenyon who now wore a sheepskin coat over his too tight suit. Guessed the ill dressed taller, thinner, older looking man at the sheriff's side would be Fletcher Grady.

Edge got to the midtown intersection at the same time as the horsemen.

'A moment of your time for a formality, Edge?' the lawman said as he reined in his horse, the other rider did likewise.

The half-breed stopped on the end of the sidewalk at the front of a two story office building that had no sidewalk on Juniper Street, but instead an outside stairway.

'Sheriff?'

'This here is Fletcher Grady, Edge.'

'How're you doing, feller?' Edge asked.

The dispirited and dishevelled man eyed the half-breed for the first time. Acknowledged the greeting with a brief nod, did not alter the expression of abject misery on his thin, unshaven, fifty-years-old face.

'Damnit, I'm not making introductions!' Kenyon snapped, and Edge thought the lawman was closer to the end of his tether than at any time during their talk in the hotel dining room.

'Not that kind of formality, uh?' Edge said.

'What?' Kenyon made a sound of impatience. 'I'm asking you if Grady looks anything at all like the man you saw at Timber Bluff this morning?'

'I wasn't nowhere near that place,' Grady growled dully, and peered directly across the intersection. Maybe looked toward the Graham Bakery beyond the theatre on the opposite corner. But probably he was just peering without seeing anything that happened to be in front of him. Because

53

the store had no living quarters out back or above it, so Roxanne Graham would not be there at this time of night. 'I ain't been out along that section of trail in more than a year. Better than two, even.'

His voice was an empty monotone that sounded as drained as he looked.

Edge reminded the lawman: 'I didn't say it was a man.'

'The Widow Graham wouldn't have done nothin' like that neither!' Grady snarled, more determined in defence of the woman than himself. His sunken eyes were briefly bright with righteous anger which he apportioned equally between the sheriff and the half-breed.

'Okay, okay!' Kenyon growled. 'I said it was just a formality. I got a duty to do, damnit!'

'And I said I wouldn't be able to recognise that rider again,' Edge said as he stepped down off the sidewalk, hung the cigarette at the corner of his mouth again.

Fletcher Grady muttered disconsolately: 'Which ain't no friggin' help to me, nor the Widow Graham nor nobody mister.'

'I'd say setting out to help people isn't something that guy makes a habit of,' Kenyon snarled, pitching his voice louder than the other man's, to make sure the sentiment was heard by the slow-walking half-breed.

Edge rasped, unheard by the others against the clop of hooves as the two men heeled their mounts across the intersection· 'I've enough bad habits I'm trying hard to break already.'

6

The Oregon Trail Saloon had seen better days, the last of which had been over many years ago.

But this was not immediately apparent from the two-story high false front which, as far as it was possible to judge in the light of the two lamps that illuminated the sign hung on an angle bracket, had been reasonably well maintained.

And as Edge pushed open the full length double doors—the batwings were not being used on a night as cold as this one—he remembered what Judge Benedict had said about the pride the people of Winton took in the appearance of the town. Although, he thought, it was probably out of a sense of discomforting shame rather than any finer feeling that Jeremiah Harman ensured that the façade of his premises was in keeping with those of the neighbouring buildings.

For in the single story building behind the false front that had recently been painted, the owner had done little or nothing to stem the ravages of time and the misuse of his saloon by what was evidently a dwindling number of patrons. In a town, the half-breed figured, that probably supported a strong temperance movement.

The bar room was a large square with wood-panelled walls and a plastered ceiling. Much beading had broken off the panels and several areas of plaster had crumbled away. At the centre of the ceiling was an unlit brass chandelier which hung lopsided and looked unsafe.

Two of the four kerosene lamps suspended above the bar along the rear wall provided a low level of illumination that left much of the squalid, cold, damp-smelling room in shadow and darkness. In their light the saloon's furnishings—chairs and tables, spittoons and a piano, the brass rail at the

55

foot of the bar and the sparsely stocked shelves along the wall behind were seen to be in keeping with the decoration of the Oregon Trail. Old and mistreated, worn out and in urgent need of repair or replacement.

Much the same could be said of the four customers. And the man behind the bar who Edge figured had to be Jeremiah Harman—the owner of the saloon who was willing to stay open late if he had the right kind of customers in his place. Customers spending money he obviously did not plough back into his business.

He was a broad-framed man of middle age with thinning black hair and a thick black beard. He looked tough at first glance, but a longer look showed his build comprised of very little muscular development. Closer to, Edge saw the man was short sighted, needed to squint to bring the world into sharp focus: which further negated the first impression of hardness.

Harman was dressed in a greasy vest, a dirty once-white shirt and a heavily stained waist apron. He had dirt under his fingernails, and a lot of other places from the smell of him.

His quartet of customers, who stood belly up to the bar in two pairs under the lighted lamps, were all older than Harman by at least ten, maybe fifteen years. They were dressed in battered hats and long, threadbare coats ill-suited for the cold night outside. Even the level of heat delivered into the large room by the potbelly stove against the side wall hung with smoke-darkened paintings of mountain scenes. A second stove against the other wall near the piano was not burning.

'What can I get you, Mr Edge?' the bartender asked eagerly, used a grubby piece of tattered cloth to wipe down an area of counter top where Edge stood between the two pairs of old-timers. The top was free of dust but much scarred by stains and burns.

The other customers, each of them with a part-drunk glass of now flat beer in front of him, had glanced at the newcomer when he first came in, showed scant interest in him before they turned to gaze across the counter again. Perhaps studied their own reflections in the aged mirror behind the bare shelves: more likely allowed their imaginations to display something more entertaining than their life-wearied faces.

'Rye whiskey.'

'The best?'

'How much better is that than the worst, feller?'

Harman smiled briefly, showing gapped and discoloured teeth. 'Two cents a shot better.'

Edge nodded. 'Okay, I figure I can afford the best. Much obliged.'

There were just a half dozen bottles and an assortment of glasses of various shapes and sizes on one shelf. The bartender reached down one of the four bottles part filled with dark-coloured liquor, and a shot glass. He put the bottle down on the counter and uncorked it, used the cloth to wipe the inside of the glass. As he made to lift the bottle and pour, Edge gripped his wrist to halt the move, told him evenly:

'I'll take care of that, okay?'

Harman pulled a face that was a mix of alarm and anger, then shrugged his meaty shoulders, said: 'Suit yourself, mister.'

'Usually do,' Edge said, and released his hold on the man.

He first sniffed the contents of the uncorked bottle, his impassive features not conveying any opinion. Then he poured whiskey into the glass until it was half full, turned it upside down in the palm of his hand and shook it. Captured the intrigued attention of the other customers as he turned, moved a few paces and continued to rinse the whiskey around in the glass. Until he emptied it into the nearest spittoon.

After the half-breed returned to the bar, set down the glass, poured a full measure and wiped his liquor-wet hand down his pants, Jeremiah Harman growled sourly:

'I hope you're going to pay for what you wasted, mister?'

'I always pay my way, feller,' Edge promised, which drew a longer-lasting smile from the bearded man. 'It wasn't wasted, though. Prevention's better than cure is what they say. In the long run, I figure it's cheaper. Don't want to catch anything worse than a cold coming out tonight.'

Harman scowled, but did not feel slighted enough to keep the expression in place for more than a few moments.

One of his customers started to laugh, which was forced to an end by a consumptive-sounding fit of coughing. Then he managed to splutter: 'He's sure got this place taped as the kinda sewer a man can catch all kinds of diseases in, uh Jeremiah?'

The bartender growled without rancour: 'You figurin' it for a sewer, Bart: that why a rat like you keeps comin' in here?'

The man with Bart muttered: 'It sure gets to smell like a sewer sometimes.'

'That'll be on account of all the shit gets talked in here,' Harman said.

'That sure is the truth,' somebody else said in a tone that suggested he considered it was a profound statement.

Edge was as unsuitably clothed for the cold as the rest of the men, and he had carried the bottle and glass to the table nearest the stove that had a glow in the grate. By the time he was seated, cigarette in one hand, shot glass of whiskey in the other, the Oregon Trail Saloon had become as quiet as when he entered.

Which brand of comfortable silence in the uncomfortable surroundings of the cold and ill-lit bar room endured for something close to thirty minutes. While he drank three and a half shots of whiskey, rolled and smoked two further cigarettes.

He felt no more at peace with himself here than in the Winton Hotel which was so luxurious by comparison. But at least here the people who shared these unprepossessing surroundings were as indifferent to him as he was to them.

They knew who he was—Harman had called him by name when he first entered the saloon—and so they certainly knew something about him showing up in town with the judge who was destined to be dead within hours. And since there was a crumpled copy of the latest edition of the *Winton Examiner* on the bartop, they surely knew just why Benedict had been shot.

But no one was interested enough to ask him any questions. Maybe just did not give a damn. It didn't matter why they were disinclined to confirm or deny the rumours they had heard. Whether it was because they were simply not the kind to interfere in something not their concern. Or they elected to ignore him because of the way he had come into the Oregon Trail, gotten what he wanted and gone to sit apart from everyone else; thus signalled his wish to be left alone. And they respected this: that a man could sometimes feel the need of only his own company.

No, he didn't give a shit for their reasons. It was a step in the right direction down the road to the kind of life he was searching for. It was the way it always used to be before...

He ended the long silence in the saloon: vented an involuntary sound, not very loud, that was a kind of half choked laugh, half angry growl.

'Something, Mr Edge?' Harman asked.

Edge swung his head toward the bartender, who had interrupted his reading of the newspaper, was looking toward him expectantly.

The other four customers, shoulders hunched, continued to give their attention to whatever images they saw in the flyblown and cracked mirror.

'Nothing,' the half-breed muttered, put his back to the spartan, unclean, ill-lit saloon again. Directed a soured smile at the battered stove as he reflected on what he had just realised.

He smiled because it was pleasing to have made the discovery that would solve, in part, what had been bothering him so much recently. The smile was soured because he had to acknowledge it meant he was destined never to find what he was looking for.

He was looking for the past: searching for a place in a time that no longer existed. Except as it was embodied in time-ravaged places like the Oregon Trail Saloon: stale, anachronistic leftovers from another decade. Clinging on to survival against the odds in smart-looking towns where otherwise upright citizens had so little of interest in their own lives that they got their pleasures from sticking their bored noses in the business of others. Particularly strangers: especially if those strangers did not match up to their exacting standards.

He allowed his mind free rein along this embittered line of thought as he slowly drank another shot of whiskey. Then decided that more liquor mixed with the inevitable conclusion he was going to reach would bring on a blacker mood. Which was not a good state of mind to encourage.

Or he could end up getting drunk. And despite the new realisation, he still felt—like he had told Mary Henderson—he had no good reason to get drunk.

So he stoppered the bottle, swallowed the heeltaps in his glass and rose from the table: went toward the bar with the bottle and glass. Glanced toward the doors of the saloon as they were flung open and three men burst noisily inside, convulsed with laughter, like one of them had gotten to the punch line of a joke as they reached the Oregon Trail.

The half-breed recognised the newcomers as fellow guests from the hotel, then looked at the saloonkeeper as a broad smile spread across his bearded face while he squinted at the drummers, saw money on the hoof.

For a moment the four old-timers at the bar counter were irritated by the bothersome interruption to their quiet drinking. But this was displaced by pleasure when Harman greeted:

'Well now, if it ain't Mr Shannon, Mr Drew and Mr Elrick, boys! Maybe we'll have us a party night at long last, uh?'

'Isn't there always that when we three hit town together, Jeremiah?' one of the happy trio countered.

One of the others had trouble controlling his laughter, then managed to force out between giggles: 'Set 'em up for everybody, Jeremiah!'

Then, abruptly, nothing was funny any longer. As, along with the eldest of the three the tallest one peered quizzically at the drummer with slicked-down hair. Saw he was glowering at Edge as the half-breed reached the bar, asked of Harman:

'How much for what I've taken out of the bottle, feller?'

Edge had a mirror image of the scene just inside the threshold of the saloon. Unclear because of the state of the mirror and the low level of light that reached that far. But clear enough.

'Roy?' the tallest of the trio asked, suddenly nervous.

'Aw shit, Barny!' the eldest muttered, disappointed that the party spirit was gone. 'It's that guy Roy figures is trying to cut him out with the girl at the hotel.'

'Call it a buck, okay?' Harman told Edge quickly, anxious to end business-losing trouble before it could get started. 'Fair to both of us, uh?'

'I'll go along with that,' Edge said, put down a dollar on the bartop as the men by the door went into a huddle, entered into a rasping exchange.

A decision was reached, a course of action agreed, before the half-breed turned from the bar counter, started toward the doorway. For the three city-suited drummers broke from the huddle and formed a short line that was long enough to block his way to the door.

Edge moved to within six feet of them, halted. Looked impassively at Roy who was between his friends, his dark eyes filled with the same brand of hostility that had emanated at the hotel.

'I don't want no trouble in my place!' Harman said, a little squeakily. In a tone that suggested he was certain he was going to get trouble and knew there was nothing he could personally do to prevent it if words were not enough. And he was sure they would not be.

'I'm not looking for trouble, Jeremiah,' Roy said. And in his tone and sneering expression, the expressions of the men who flanked him, there was self-possessed confidence they could handle it with consummate ease if necessary.

Edge said flatly: 'You fellers don't step aside, you're looking *at* it.'

Barny, who was the tallest and broadest of the three, said in a monotone: 'You don't need to talk tough, Edge. Me and Roy and Glen run up against your type all the time on our sales trips round the country. We know you're no milksop, mister.'

'That's right!' Glen growled. At forty, he was perhaps five years older than the others. Like Roy, he was not so much shorter and lighter than Barny. 'Most times we find it easier to step aside, back down when your kind acts as tough as they talk.'

'But you can see you're outnumbered here, mister!' Roy pointed out. 'And this is different from usual. So you best listen to what I'm going to tell you. And do like I tell you.'

Barry reinforced the warning: 'Because we can outnumber you again if there's need.'

'That's right,' Glen agreed. And just for a second when his gaze was trapped by the glittering, ice cold stare in the slitted eyes of the half-breed, he was afraid. His loose dentures, which clacked when he talked, now rattled as he swallowed hard.

Edge shifted his gaze to Roy without altering the icy expression in his eyes, invited: 'Get said what's on your mind, feller.'

Roy nodded, snapped: 'I saw you making time with Miss Henderson at the hotel. I know you know I saw you.'

'Saw you didn't like it when she talked with me,' Edge replied evenly.

'Nor the way you looked at her, mister! I don't want it to happen again. I want you to steer clear of her. Miss Henderson and me, we're pretty close to having an understanding, okay?'

'It's fine with me,' Edge drawled. 'And I'd guess she's of an age when you don't have to get her parents' permiss——'

'You know what I mean, damnit!'

'They got to act tough all the time, his type,' Barny growled.

Edge started to say: 'Something that would be okay with me is——'

'I don't give a shit what's okay or not with you, mister!' Roy snarled.

Edge completed: '... if you'll step out of my way so I can leave.'

'I don't want no trouble here in my place, Edge,' Jeremiah Harman felt it necessary to repeat when he detected a slight hardening of the half-breed's tone.

'Nor neither do we, mister,' one of the old-timers at the bar augmented. 'These gents are friends of ours and we——'

He was shushed into silence by the other old men, who were not so sure of the wisdom of involving themselves for the sake of a couple of free drinks supplied by the on-the-town drummers.

'Fine,' Roy said. 'Just don't let me hear you been trying to make time with Miss Henderson no more, okay?'

He almost smiled as he relished a sense of triumph at the outcome of the confrontation.

Edge shook his head slowly: as slowly as he raised his right hand to tug at his right earlobe with the forefinger and thumb. Said evenly: 'You people have caught me at a bad time.'

'Same as with okay, mister,' the increasingly confident Roy growled. 'I don't give a shit what kind of time you're having.'

Barny laughed hollowly, said: 'So long as it's not time you're making with Roy's girl!'

Edge's hand moved from his ear into the long hair at the nape of his neck. Like he was going to scratch himself. But it did not move back and forth in any kind of scratching motion. Instead, it came out of his hair, clenched into a fist, in a blur of speed. The glint of something metallic was momentarily visible at one side.

There were gasps, curses, small cries of alarm. From the drummers and the men at the bar.

Then backing off in unison by the trio aligned across the double doorway.

Edge lunged forward, thrust his right arm out to the right. Then swung it to the left. At the end of each of these moves he made a short downward arc with his fisted hand. Between them twisted his wrist. So that the finely-honed blade of the straight razor was aimed at its target, penetrated deeply into the flesh, erupted enough blood to shock everyone into a brief period of stupefied paralysis. And leave scars that would stay with the victim for a long time: maybe for life.

'Roy?' Barny squealed.

'Oh, my God!' Glen rasped, hardly more than a whisper.

Roy began to express anger at being cut. A moment later experienced terror as he became aware of how badly he was hurt, felt the vast quantity of warm blood that spurted out of the three inch wounds inscribed across both cheeks. From close to the corners of his eyes almost to the sides of his mouth.

'Wha... what...?' he began to stutter as he stared fixedly

63

at the razor that was dripping his blood, tightly clenched in the blood stained fist of the half-breed.

Edge transferred the razor to his left hand, wiped the blood off the back of his right hand on his pants leg as he reached for the butt of the Frontier Colt jutting out of the holster. He touched the revolver with just his fingertips as he said:

'In the circumstances, I figured I asked politely. Now, unless you fellers want to find out how much more trouble you're looking at, you better move your asses clear of the way I want to go.'

'God, I gotta sit down,' Roy whimpered, pressed both hands hard against his cheeks, but failed to stem the flow of blood which squeezed through the cracks between his fingers.

'Sure,' Barny said, took a tight grip on the man's upper arm and steered him to the nearest table, dragged out a chair and guided him gently down on to it.

The half-breed grunted his satisfaction, folded the blade into the handle of the razor and returned it to the pouch at the nape of his neck.

Glen sidestepped nervously toward the other two drummers, grimaced at the half-breed as he asked hoarsely: 'That's the reason you're called Edge, I guess?'

'I'm called Edge because that's the name I was given, feller,' he told the man as he gripped the doorknob. It was close enough to the truth for this occasion.

'There was no call to go as far as you did, mister!' one of the old-timers at the bar complained. 'Ain't nobody else in here armed. Them guys would've backed off if you'd just pulled that gun of yours on 'em!'

He was shushed into silence as Edge answered:

'He should remember what a bad mistake he made with me.'

'He'll do that sure enough,' Barny muttered bitterly: grimaced as he pulled away one of Roy's bloodrun hands, saw the seriousness of the gaping wound he knew was matched by another on the other cheek.

'Right,' Edge said. 'And he should know there was no need for it. I don't have on the girl any of what I carved on him.'

'What the frig are you talking about, you sonofabitch?'

Roy groaned, covering both sides of his face again.

Edge pulled open the door, told him evenly: 'Designs.'

Edge spoke the absolute truth as he stepped out of the malodorous Oregon Trail Saloon, closed the double doors and moved along the empty street, across the timber bridge over the Beaver River and down toward the intersection.

The clean smelling night air was colder than before and the sky was pricked by stars and slashed by a sliver of new moon that glinted in a way that suggested a frost before morning.

He suddenly felt good to have made the discovery concerning the kind of compromises he was going to have to make if he hoped to achieve the kind of life he wanted to lead.

He had been a realist for too long to think of attempting the patently impossible: the clock could not be turned back.

It was a bonus to have proved by a practical demonstration that he could still handle trouble in his old way. But he did not invite a switch back to a dark mood by wondering how long this could continue.

So, he had a contented mind as he reached the midtown intersection of Winton's two main streets. Accompanied by a full belly and a pleasant glow from the liquor. His trail supplies were all bought, and after some sleep which would probably not last long because of the way he had bedded down in the afternoon, he could make an early start.

And if there was a sparkling frost covering the night country under a bright sky, so much the better to light his way south until the new day dawned.

Beyond the intersection, the eastern length of Juniper was as deserted as this stretch he was on. The only pool of bright light which fell across the sidewalk down there was from the window of the law office. Where the horses of Sheriff Kenyon and Fletcher Grady were still hitched to the rail outside.

Which maybe meant the lawman and the suspect were still talking and there was a chance Grady would not be arrested and locked up.

Which was no concern of the half-breed, he realised: and directed a stream of saliva on to the street as he turned the corner. Saw the entire length of Travis was empty, too, with fewer glimmers of light escaping from draped windows than earlier.

He could understand why few hotel guests ever required keys so they could stay out late in this town.

The livery stable was right next door to the hotel. The forge was on the other side of the street, further south. Both were locked up tight for the night and there was no living accommodation out back of either of the timber built, single story premises that smelled of horses and saddlesoap, horses and cold ashes. Neither building had a sign on its double doors to show where the liveryman or the blacksmith lived.

The hotel was still open for present guests, and new ones in the unlikely event any transients showed up in Winton at this time of night. The lamps in the lobby were dimmed and the kitchen and dining room were totally darkened: just a faint trace of supper and the perfume of rich old ladies still lingering in the stove-warmed air.

Voices sounded from behind a door marked *Private* behind the check-in desk. He guessed the Henderson family lived beyond the door and he went toward it. He intended to knock, ask whoever opened it if they would direct him to where the men he wanted lived. So he could make arrangements to leave early, pay what he owed before he rode out of town.

But the door was wrenched violently open before he was halfway across the lobby from the hotel entrance. And Mary Henderson stepped hurriedly out, her head craned around to peer back inside. She rasped grimly, her voice tremulous with emotion:

'I'm a full grown adult woman! Plenty old enough to choose my own friends, thank you very much!'

'But Mary, I only mean to——' her father started to explain.

'Leave it for now, dear,' his wife tried to placate.

Their daughter banged the door closed, spun around, froze with a tiny choked cry trapped in her throat. The high colour of her anger got even higher from embarrassment when she saw Edge. She opened her mouth to say something, then snapped her head around to stare at the firmly closed door: seemed not to trust herself to say anything in case it should bring her parents outside to prolong the family squabble.

Instead, she put a forefinger to her lips and beckoned vigorously to Edge, went across the lobby and started up the elegant curve of the stairway. He followed, heeding her emphatic signal to be quiet until they were halfway to the top. Then he drawled:

'Much as I like being invited upstairs by a lovely young lady, Miss Henderson, I'd——'

'It's exactly what you hope it is, Mr Edge,' she broke in tautly, without turning to look back at him. There was a tone of resolute determination in her voice that did not go well with what he had believed was her subject. But this softened when she added: 'I hope you'll continue to like it.'

She reached the door of his room, used the pass key from a pocket in her dress to unlock it. She stepped into the room that was not large, took just three paces before she came up against the side of the bed. Where she turned to look at him standing in the doorway: a silhouette against the light from the hallway that filtered in and showed she now wore an expression that was not at all embarrassed: was still a little angry, though.

'It's all right,' she assured, slightly anxious. 'I was married once, so you won't be spoiling anything that's supposed to be precious to a woman.'

He recalled what he had told the men in the saloon about not having any designs on this woman. Then dismissed the men from his mind. Thought instead about his intention to ask any member of the Henderson family about where to find the blacksmith and the liveryman. Sent this notion the way of that concerned with the Oregon Trail. Received a vivid memory of how he felt as he left the dining room, when her smile of invitation triggered his arousal.

By this time he had stepped over the threshold, closed the door at his back. Could still see her dimly, as she could see him, in the moon and starlight that gleamed at the small window, patterned by the net curtain that hung there.

'One question?' he said.

'Whatever you want. I've got all night.' She shrugged. 'If that's what you want?'

'I'm happy I won't be spoiling anything. But I'd like to know why you're spoiling me this way?'

'It's personal,' she replied shortly, with a note of finality that demanded he ask no more questions on that subject.

Edge allowed a sigh to whistle out through his pursed lips, muttered as he moved toward the woman waiting beside the bed: 'Yeah, I guess there's not much that's more personal than this.'

He scaled his hat on to the top of his gear heaped in a corner of the room. Put his arms around her slender but pleasingly curved body. Smelled her hair and the crisp cleanness of a dress that was not the black and white one she wore earlier.

Her breath was sweet enough to make him uncomfortably aware of the whiskey fumes he breathed at her as he pressed his lips to hers. Thought for a moment that her rigid resistance was a reaction to this. But when he cracked open his eyes, he saw hers were enlarged by shock: like she only now realised what she was getting into and was afraid, desperately wanted to end it here.

In that instant he did not know if he would have allowed her to do this. But then it no longer was an issue. Because her eyes softly closed and her body was yielding as she brought up her arms to embrace him. Then both of them were enclosed in that near ecstasy of pleasure when everything outside their own intimate experiences was beyond the reach of sensation.

While the kiss went on, he began to unfasten the buttons at the back of her dress and she moaned at the brushing touch of his fingertips across her bare flesh. Moments later, as his hands moved down her back far enough so the smooth silken fabric of an undergarment came between his hands and her skin, she made a dissatisfied sound, freed her embrace, withdrew her lips from his and whispered:

'I'll do it, please? You take your clothes off?'

There was apology in her soft voice. Then urgent hurry in her movements as she completed what he had started. Looked at him just once, anxiety changing to an eager smile when she saw he was doing what she asked.

She finished first. And without looking at him, pulled back the covers, got in to the narrow bed and uttered a deep-throated sound that could have been of delicious anticipation or maybe was triggered by the sudden coldness of the sheets against her flesh.

Edge only glimpsed her pale nakedness for a second before she jerked the covers to her chin. And beyond the wedge of light from the window her head was just a patch of darkness on the white of the pillow.

He heard her breathing deeply and regularly and sometimes sensed her eyes upon him: more often not. He continued to undress without haste, so he would not seem fumblingly eager to possess her willing body.

When he was naked, he turned toward the bed, heard her vent a gasp of shock. Or perhaps it was a sound of embarrassment. And she wrenched her head to the side, like she didn't want him to know she had been gazing hungrily at his powerfully built, potently male body with its ridges of muscles and many scars of ancient bullet wounds.

Then it was his turn to be disconcerted: as the temperature in the unheated room reduced his thrusting want to a flaccid, useless thing: was relieved she did not see this as he lay down beside her on the narrow bed.

She shivered as his coldness was transmitted to her flesh, warmed by the half minute or so she had been in bed.

'There is a good reason,' she told him, shivered again as she responded to the pressure of his body and the process began to be reversed: her body heat started to warm him as he reached an arm across her, cupped a smooth and firm shoulder in his palm.

'There doesn't have to be,' he told her. 'But if it's what you want, that's fine with me.'

'Let's not talk now,' she whispered, and brought up a hand

to lay fingers gently on the centre of his mouth. A moment later moved the hand, hooked it behind his neck and pulled his head down to press his lips to her own.

His arousal stirred against her thigh. Moved more insistently when he trailed the hand from her shoulder to her breast. Found the nipple was already erected, the warmth of the mound of flesh beneath showing this had nothing to do with the cold of the night.

While her hand continued to caress the back of his head gently, prolong the kiss, the other was flat on his back. Until it began to apply a steady pressure, the fingers forming into a claw, that asked if he was as ready as she.

He submitted to what she desired, moved gently up and on to her, his legs sinking between the wide splay of her thighs. Next moved his hand from the swollen nipple, reached down between them to guide himself toward the centre of her urgent need.

But then she showed she was not yet fully ready for the final pleasure. She pulled her lips away from his and wrenched her head sideways on the pillow. Pushed forcefully at his head, demanding he replace his hand with his mouth on her breast.

He continued to do as she wanted. Needed to arch his lower body up from her so he was able to take the nipple and the summit of her breast into his mouth, tease it with his tongue without removing his stiffened, stirring, straining want away from the hirsute triangle he could feel was already moist.

She could endure this degree of pleasure for only a few moments. Then moaned, muttered words that were incomprehensible but conveyed an obvious meaning, arched her body to press her readiness against him. Hugged his head into the crook of her neck again, moaned as his teeth dug gently into her flesh. Moaned more deeply as he impaled her body, sank slowly inside her in a manner that sent a tremor through her entire being.

Then there was just the sounds of their breath, sucked in and expelled at a cadence that matched the thrust and withdrawal: flesh in flesh, body against body. Her legs spread wider, until her feet slapped on the floor at either side of the

71

bed. Her belly arched hard up to his, desperate to take in the last fraction of an inch of him. Her arms were flung far to the side, hands splayed in an attitude of total submission.

She finished seconds before he did, her legs and arms suddenly limp. But she continued to arch her body to his, drawing from deep within a reserve of strength as her every pore oozed sweat, her breathing got faster and louder while her mouth gaped wide, her eyes squeezed tightly closed in the struggle not to submit to the demand for rest that her body implored.

Finally he emptied into her, and she vented a choked cry of pain as, for a second, exhaustion caused Edge to sprawl the full weight of his drained frame on top of her.

'I'm real sorry,' he murmured, rose up from her, and slid out of the bed so she could bring her legs under the covers, the sweat on them suddenly icy cold.

'Not for the rest of what happened, I hope?' she asked breathlessly as she watched him go through the untidy pile of his clothing.

He pulled his longjohns free and put them on, covering his own flesh that was goose bumped by coldly drying sweat.

'That's for sure,' he told her.

'But you're getting dressed? Does that mean you don't want me to stay all night with you?'

'It's cold in here.'

'It's warm in here.'

He showed a smile that revealed his teeth gleaming in the light that was not bright enough to let her see there was no mirth in his slitted eyes when he said: 'That bed just ain't big enough for the both of us, ma'am. When it's sleep we're in need of.'

'Yes, I know. But it's your bed. I'm the one that ought to——'

'In awhile maybe,' he interrupted, pulled on his pants and draped the sheepskin coat over his shoulders. Then he sat on the hard-seated, straight-backed chair that with a closet, a small table and the bed comprised the room's spartan but adequate furnishings.

'Or we could go to one of the doubles,' she suggested eagerly.

'Couple of things I'd like to ask you?' he said.

She made a sound of annoyance, then sighed, rolled her head on the pillow so she was peering at the ceiling immediately above her. Wrongly anticipated his questions when she said: 'You can thank my parents for the unexpected pleasure I hope you just had?'

'It's the most pleasure I've had since the last time I had the pleasure,' he responded to her implied request for reassurance. Decided that if Mary Henderson now needed to talk for awhile, he could wait that long before asking where the liveryman and the blacksmith lived.

'You see, my father especially has gotten to be real concerned about the kind of men I like since Mal Schultz ran off and left me.'

'He was the young man you were married to?'

'Right. Still am, I guess. Unless he died. They warned me not to marry him. Said he'd only cause me grief and heartache, and they were sure right about that. He stayed with me for just two months before he took off. Stole the money and my mother's jewellery and some valuables belonged to guests that was all in the hotel safe. Ever since that happened, my parents get nervous whenever I show an interest in any man who they figure reminds them of Mal.'

Edge moved to go to his clothes on the floor again, and she said irritably:

'I'm sorry if this is boring you!'

'Feel the need of a smoke is all,' he told her evenly as he took the makings from a pocket of his shirt and sat on the chair again.

She still sounded a little miffed when she said: 'Aren't you going to ask which man reminded them of Mal this time, Edge?'

'I guess I know, Miss Henderson, unless I just got lucky when I showed up in the hotel lobby when I did?'

'No, you did not just get lucky!' She was close to indignant anger at the implication that any man would have served to get back at her parents. She needed a few moments to suppress the unwanted emotion.

Edge reminded her: 'The way we got off on the wrong foot right after the judge was shot?'

73

'The way you were about that, it shocked me. But it's the way you are. Later though, I tried to show you——'

'You showed me a nice smile, Miss Henderson,' he cut in. 'But that could have been just because I happened to——'

'Yes, I can see that,' she said quickly. 'And you did happen to be around at the right time, it must be admitted. But it was *you*. No other man would have...'

'Okay, Miss Henderson.'

'What?' She snapped her head up from the pillow to peer at him, afraid he was acknowledging a decision he had just made rather than responding to what she had said.

'I know what you mean,' he amplified. And he did, from experience. For she was not the first woman to be repelled by him at first, then inexorably attracted to him.

His tone was even and his features were impassive. She continued to look hard at him for a stretched second, decided to accept the comment at face value: not to consider it a veiled hint he was growing impatient with her. She said:

'My father... Well, maybe it wouldn't have been such an issue this time if one of the travelling men who stays at the hotel regularly hadn't been around tonight. My father has a high regard for men in permanent employment. Especially if they are neat dressers and only travel to do their jobs. They aren't rootless and don't carry guns.'

This last she said in a rush. He replied in the same neutral tone as before while he rolled the paper around the line of tobacco: 'Guess I can understand why a father should think that way, ma'am. But I'm grateful you disagree with him.'

'Yes, so can I understand,' she said quickly, ignoring his second comment. 'If I was looking for a husband. But having being married to somebody like Mal, I'm not looking for another one. At least, not yet. Right now, all I want is to...'

She left the sentence unfinished as he struck a match on the underside of the chair seat and the flare seemed to be inordinately brilliant in the small room. Turned her face sharply away from the bright flame, perhaps more in embarrassment at the point she was trying to make than because the light hurt her eyes.

'Oh, I must sound like a——' This time she broke off

because she couldn't bring herself to apply such a term to herself.

'You were married,' Edge helped her out on an expelled stream of tobacco smoke. 'You liked that part of being married as much as most people do. That's only natural, seems to me. But in a town like Winton, unattached ladies aren't supposed to——'

She vented a disdainful snort, hurried to explain: 'Don't you believe it!'

She seemed surprised at the degree of venom in this bald statement that poured scorn on a section of her fellow citizens. Moderated her tone to add: 'Well, all right. Such women aren't supposed to do anything about taking care of their natural needs. I guess most of them don't. But plenty do.'

She pulled a face, shrugged in the bed, allowed: 'I don't suppose Winton is so different from any other town like it. What goes on behind closed doors that sometimes aren't closed that tight, well... Well, let me tell you, Edge. Take poor Judge Benedict, for instance. It's not just the widow of his old friend he called on when he came to town who'll miss him so badly now he's gone. The judge used to visit quite a few ladies around here, so it won't just be Mrs Hussy who'll——'

She broke off with a soft cry and shook her head in a gesture of self-disgust, muttered: 'But this is stupid. You don't want to listen to small town gossip. I'm ashamed of myself for indulging in it. More ashamed of that than for what we just did: for being here with you like this.'

She raised her head to peer down over the covers contouring her naked body.

Edge took the cigarette from his mouth to say: 'I don't think there's any reason why you should be ashamed, Miss Henderson.'

'You know what I think?' She smiled briefly. 'I think us being here like this, after we did what we did together, that it would be all right for you to call me Mary. Don't you agree? And I'd like to call you something other than Edge?'

'Like I told somebody in the saloon tonight, Mary, Edge is

my name. For a long time it's the only one I've had.'

'What?' She shrugged again, decided not to pursue the matter of his name as something else he said caught her interest. 'Oh, I guess you saw Roy Elrick and his two friends at the Oregon Trail? He's the one has my parent's seal of approval as somebody I should be interested in.'

There was disdain in her tone, which developed into a more powerful emotion when Edge said flatly:

'He sounded pretty confident about putting his brand on you.'

'Oh?' She was bristling with rage, conveyed with the monosyllable exclamation a far deeper brand of anger at the drummer than she had harboured for her father. 'He was boasting about me, was he?'

'He didn't say too much about you,' Edge told her. 'I cut him short.'

She peered at the half-breed through the darkness of the room now aromatic with tobacco smoke. Obviously was about to press for more details, until Edge spoke first.

'That couple of things I wanted to ask you about?'

'Yes?' She uttered another sound of self-deprecation. 'Oh, you didn't want to hear all about me and my troubles! Damn! I can be so selfish sometimes!'

'No sweat,' he said lightly. 'Like they say, you bestowed your favours on me, Mary. So I did you the favour of listening to you when you needed to talk up a storm. Makes me even. Unless you want repaying for some information.'

'Information?'

'Just like to know where I can find the liveryman and the blacksmith now their businesses are closed up for the day?'

'Mr O'Mally and Mr Craig? Yes, of course I can tell you where they live. Guests of the hotel sometimes need their services late in the day. But I don't know if they'd welcome being disturbed at this time of night.'

The grandfather clock in the lobby sounded distant chimes to mark the lateness of the hour as she spoke. Edge did not count how many times it struck: at least ten or eleven. He reminded her:

'It wasn't this late when I was first going to ask.'

76

'You surely don't want to leave town right now, though?'

'Want to pay for the livery service and two new shoes. Fix it to get my horse out of the stable if it's not open before dawn. Guess those fellers would like being woken up early about as much as this late?'

He abruptly felt dissatisfied, a little irritated with himself. Realised this was caused by having to discuss such mundane details while he sat half dressed in this cold bedroom and a warm and willing woman lay in his bed.

'Oh, that's easily solved, she assured him. 'There's a list of their charges at the desk. You just pay me what's owed and I'll see Mr Craig and Mr O'Mally get the money.'

'Fine,' he reached into a back pocket of his pants, drew out some bills and looked questioningly at her.

She hooked a hand over the top of the bedcovers, raised them slightly, said seductively: 'But it's not that urgent, surely. Maybe we could make it so you'll sleep in late? If you'll do me another favour of allowing me to bestow my favours on——'

She was smiling until a woman screamed. It was a keening, drawn out sound from along the second floor hallway toward the head of the stairs. A sound that held to a high pitch for stretched seconds, then wailed into abrupt silence.

This silence lasted for perhaps three seconds as Edge remained frozen in the process of removing the cigarette from his mouth to respond to the invitation. And Mary Henderson dropped her hand, put out the other alongside it and jerked the covers to her chin: like she registered the scream as some kind of condemnation of her nakedness.

Then she gasped.

Edge hung the cigarette back at the side of his mouth.

The woman who had screamed now shouted in a terrified voice: 'It's Mr McCormack! Bill, come quick! Mr McCormack's been killed!'

'That's mother!' Mary Henderson rasped in a hushed whisper, threw off the covers and scrambled out of bed, unconcerned about her nakedness as she snatched up her clothes.

'Who's McCormack?' Edge asked against a rising volume

of vocal noise and thudding footfalls much the same as the body of sound triggered by the shooting of Judge Benedict.

'Warner McCormack's one of our resident guests,' she said breathlessly as, awkward with haste, she struggled into her clothes. 'He's been in bed, sick with the 'flu, for a week. One of us always brings him his medicine last thing each night. Poor mother, finding him dead.'

Edge stood up, shrugged the sheepskin coat from his shoulders, and began to unfasten his pants. Wondered indifferently if she had failed to make the distinction between McCormack being killed and found dead.

Then she paused in buttoning her dress, stared at him as he started to get undressed again. Demanded huskily: 'What are you doing?'

'Getting ready to bed down,' he told her evenly.

'But what about...?' Aren't you going to...? The way mother screamed, it doesn't seem like Mr McCormack died from the 'flu.'

He told her: 'Right, she said killed. I've seen a lot of bodies that got to be dead for all sorts of reasons. So——'

'But surely you——'

'It's none of my concern,' he cut in and there was a hard tone in his voice that triggered a small cry of shock or even alarm from her.

She began again to fumble with the fastenings of her clothing, all the time directing bleak glances at him that tacitly accused him of falling way short of the standards she had assumed for him.

Then there was an explosion.

It shook the walls and ceiling, rattled the window of the room. Triggered shrieks of terror from out of the less strident babble of fear that had previously sounded throughout the hotel.

And Mary Henderson hurled herself at Edge, her arms flung wide, then closing to wrap tightly around him. He instinctively embraced her as she clung to him, trembling with fear.

'Dear God, what was that?' she rasped.

'Something that went bump in the night,' he growled.

'I've got to go see!' she insisted, broke from him and turned to the door.

She wrenched it open, lunged out over the threshold and thudded into an elderly woman who was as anxious as she was to find out what was happening.

'I'm so sorry, Mrs Corbett-Webb!' Mary called back as she broke into a run along the hallway.

Mrs Corbett-Webb, who Edge recalled seeing in the dining room at suppertime, had draped a topcoat around her shoulders over her nightdress. She was winded and incensed by the collision as she sagged back against the wall opposite the open door. Peered angrily for several moments after the retreating form of Mary Henderson. Then glanced into the room, did a double-take when she saw Edge in process of getting dressed beside the rumpled bed, gasped:

'Well, I never!'

'Then you should try it, ma'am,' the half-breed replied evenly. 'But you should know the earth don't move that much with every bang.'

8

By the time Edge was fully dressed, complete with sheepskin coat and gunbelt, the holster tied down to his right thigh, it sounded like the entire population of Winton had spilled out on to the streets.

Which was understandable, for it was inevitable the death of a hotel guest was of less general interest than the massive explosion: and the raging fire it had apparently started, from the acrid taint of smoke that was even discernible in the air along the second floor hallway.

This hallway was empty when he stepped out of his room, started toward the head of the stairs. He paused there when a nearby door opened and Kath Henderson came out, pale faced, red eyed and tremulous with shock. Her scowling husband emerged behind her and closed the door quietly, like somebody within the room was sleeping far less lightly than Warner McCormack.

The woman brought a hand to her throat quickly, blurted: 'Oh, Mr Edge. What an awful thing to happen? Mr McCormack was such a good and fine gentleman.'

The bony hand moved from her pulsing throat, bunched into a loose fist, and she rubbed the knuckles across her eyes, like she was trying to erase the signs of grief for a man she had so much admired.

'But how many others were killed in the explosion across town, dear?' her husband asked rhetorically, directed something close to a sneer toward the half-breed.

'How did he die, ma'am?' Edge asked, gestured toward the closed door with his hand holding the cigarette butt which had gone out.

'What?' Her mind had wandered, perhaps was filled with

rueful memories of the newly dead man.

'You said he was killed and I——'

'I think it only right and proper the circumstances of Mr McCormack's death should first be conveyed to the sheriff before it becomes common gossip,' Henderson said staidly.

'Oh, don't be so vindictive, Bill!' his wife accused. 'Half the town surely knows already. Enough people saw him. Warner McCormack was throttled, Mr Edge.'

'Kath, I really think——' Henderson attempted to cut her off, fastened a grip on her upper arm.

'Strangled with one of his own cravats that's still tied around his throat,' she insisted on amplifying. But she allowed herself to be steered around Edge and down the stairs. Went on without looking back at the half-breed: 'But that isn't all. No, sir. There's a rope noose pinned to the front of his nightshirt. Just like the one was fixed to the clothing of poor Judge Benedict. Dear God in Heaven, it's all so——'

'Yes, dear,' her husband agreed, curled an arm tightly around her trembling shoulders like he thought she might stumble down the stairs. 'It's a terrible thing. Let me get you to our rooms, then I'll go tell the sheriff.'

Edge started down the stairs behind them, met with impassiveness the hostile glare Bill Henderson directed briefly back at him.

Mrs Henderson said: 'I'm sure that for the time being Mr Kenyon has more than enough on his plate with the explosion, Bill. I wonder what it was? It was so terribly loud, wasn't it?'

They reached the lobby, cold with night air that flowed in through the double doors left open by guests who had hurried outside to satisfy their curiosity about the awesome violence that shattered them awake. The smell of new burning was much stronger down here.

Henderson steered his wife toward their living quarters, telling her she should not worry about anything except getting over her shock right then. He shepherded her through their doorway behind the desk.

Edge stepped out on to the porch where most of his fellow guests, ill-attired for the frosty night in whatever items of

81

clothing came to hand to pull over their nightgowns, were huddled into a number of tightknit groups. All of them peered toward the far end of Travis Street: where a much larger throng was gathered out front of a burning building.

Edge arced away his dead cigarette butt as a man turned toward him, eager to relay information to a newcomer on the scene.

'I heard somebody say it was the newspaper building that went up. Quite some detonation, uh?'

It was the father of the young family Edge saw in the dining room. He was without his wife and two children. The topcoat draped around his shoulders was stitched with the insignia of an infantry lieutenant.

'And it's said a woman was seen running hell for leather away after the explosion,' one of the rich old ladies supplied.

She was not the one who had seen Edge, partly dressed, as Mary Henderson ran from his room. But when she saw who she was addressing—she had spoken without being aware of this, her attention was fixed on the distant fire while she passed on the sensational piece of information—she glared at the half-breed with much the same degree of animosity as had Mrs Corbett-Webb in the second floor hallway.

Now, most of the others on the porch shifted their attention from the fire to Edge. And despite the certain death of a fellow guest and destruction and possibility of more death at the far end of Travis Street, they almost all had a capacity to show a high degree of hostile resentment for him. The force of their feelings too strong to be caused by the fact of a woman being seen leaving his room.

'Sure has been a whole mess of trouble tonight, ain't there?' a man said. He was the grizzled old-timer who had brought up the hot water for Edge's morning bath, carried no grudge about anything or anyone as he shook his shaggy head, growled: 'I ain't never known Winton so stirred up.'

'Trouble is that guy's middle name, Danny,' another man muttered sourly as Edge stepped off the porch, swung past a group of four youngish men.

He looked up at them in the shadow of the porch roof, recognised Drew, Shannon and two of the other travelling salesmen peering down at him: all of them expressing the brand of disgust they probably reserved usually for something picked up on the sole of a shoe.

And he guessed one of these drummers had broadcast details of what he had done to Roy Elrick at the saloon: had naturally slanted the account so there was just the one villain. That would certainly have stirred up bad feeling against him.

Now it was one of the salesmen who had not been at the saloon who made the embittered remark: suddenly altered his expression from belligerent to fearful when Edge came to a halt, fixed him with a glinting-eyed gaze.

'The doc says Roy could be scarred for life, just like you wanted it to be,' Barny said.

'We all of us heard what you did to that poor young man!' one of the glowering old ladies rasped. 'You should be ashamed, attacking an unarmed man that way!'

There were nods and sounds of agreement with this sentiment from most of the people crowded on the porch. A few intrigued frowns on the faces of some who had not heard the story.

Edge asked evenly: 'Any of you people know a place in Winton where I can get some sackcloth?'

'What the——' one of the drummers started to snarl.

'There are ladies present, mister!' the infantry lieutenant snapped grimly.

Edge gestured along the street as he started to amble in that direction, said: 'Know where I can get the ashes, in the event I start to feel bad about Elrick.'

There was a buzz of affronted talk from the porch, but this was ended abruptly by a loud crash of falling timber from down at the end of the street. Accompanied by a massive billowing of black smoke lit by tongues of flame which drew gasps and cries of shock and horror.

The fire was roaring evenly and the shouts of those close to it had diminished by the time Edge reached the intersection. He glanced east along Juniper, saw the law office was no longer lit and the two horses were gone from the rail out front. Just as elsewhere, many house windows and open doorways threw wedges of light across sidewalks and front yards, from lamps left burning by people who had hurried out to see what caused the explosion.

He wondered idly as he started along the northern stretch of Travis if the absence of light in the law office and the vacant hitching rail meant the place was empty. If this were so—Fletcher Grady had been set free—he would certainly be the prime suspect for the second murder of the day.

But then the half-breed made the conscious effort to ignore such conjecture. For the guilt or innocence of Grady had no bearing at all on the reason he was out here on the crowded, firelit street.

The timber building in which the *Winton Examiner* was printed was two stories high. It was an old building, its frame walls seasoned to tinder dryness by the elements over countless years. And the flames were devouring it with ravenous speed despite the desperate efforts to put out the fire.

The men engaged in this task, so obviously doomed to failure, were formed into a human chain that stretched from the front of the burning building, across Travis and down a narrow side street through the poorer quarter of town. Reached to the Beaver River, from which buckets of water were scooped up and passed, hand to hand, along the line.

They did this with the well drilled expertise of men regularly trained in firefighting techniques. Were overseen by Nicholas Kenyon, who moved constantly back and forth along the line, yelling instructions, urging more speed, sometimes taking a place in the line and handling the buckets himself.

He was more than a loud voice and waving arms, though. He paid close attention to every man in the line, from time to time yelled a name which caused somebody to run out of the watching crowd, to replace a tiring link in the chain.

No one seemed to acknowledge that it was obviously a losing battle to save the building: that the raging inferno was getting worse and it almost seemed each bucket of water hurled into the flames only served to make them roar higher. As if the river water was turned by malevolent magic into kerosene as it travelled along the line of cursing, shouting, grimacing, heavily breathing men who sweated and strained, some of them closest to the fire stripped to the waist.

Overhead, beyond the reach of the thick smoke, the moon and stars gleamed with glittering intensity; emphatically warning there was no chance of the kind of downpour that had drenched this piece of the Cascades throughout last night.

If Sheriff Kenyon noticed Edge, registered who he was as he merged with the crowd of hurriedly-dressed, eager-faced watchers, he gave no sign of it. There was no reason why he should, of course, for even if the trouble at the Oregon Trail had been reported to him—and if so many of the hotel guests knew of it, surely he did?—this was neither the time nor the place to deal with the aftermath of a saloon brawl.

Edge saw Jeremiah Harman in the line, three of the old-timers who had been patrons of the saloon in the watching group.

He failed to see the liveryman who had taken his horse from him this morning: did not know what the blacksmith looked like. And was about to ask if anyone had seen O'Mally or Craig on the firelit street when he spotted Mary Henderson.

The woman saw him at the same moment, stiffened and glowered, then started to force a way resolutely through the press of people toward him. Her aggressive expression became more hard set the closer she got to where he waited.

'You didn't go back to bed then?' she rasped, her voice low but mouthing the words emphatically so he might read her lips in the constantly leaping and writhing fireglow if the sound of the raging flames masked what she said.

He told her: 'It seemed like a good chance to square myself with O'Mally and Craig without having to wake them. You seen either of those——'

'I heard what you did to Roy Elrick!' she snarled, and the way she deliberately shaped her lips acted to stress the hostility of her expression. 'When I came out of the hotel, his friends were there and they told——'

It explained the animosity of most of the people grouped on the hotel porch. He nodded, said: 'Yeah, I know. But that

85

doesn't have anything to do with me trying to find the blacksmith and the——'

'I know Roy well enough to think of him as a good friend, Edge!'

'That's more or less what he told me, Mary. What I don't know is where to——'

'And after what you'd done to him, you let me——'

Edge interrupted her again, with undisguised impatience now: 'It seemed like it was you let me, as I recall.'

The front wall of the newspaper building collapsed and they were forced back with the crowd as a billowing wind of searing heat exploded across the street.

'Don't get smart with me, Edge!' she snarled softly. 'If I'd known what kind of man you really are—it wasn't just a tough act you put on to try to impress me after the judge was killed—I wouldn't have...'

She looked about to hurl herself at him: fists flying or hands clawed maybe. To hurt him in retaliation for what he did to Elrick. Or what she had let him do to her while she knew nothing of the drummer's injuries. But then she held her hands up in front of her face, fingers splayed, grimaced at them and shuddered as she said: 'God, I feel like I've got blood on *my* hands from just letting you touch me! I just don't know how you could do that to somebody and almost the next minute take me to your bed and be so... So——'

'It's all part of the cut and thrust of daily life, Mary,' he said.

'You... You...' If her temper had been a degree hotter she would probably have spat an obscenity at him. Instead she finished lamely: 'You disgust me! You're nothing but a good for noth——'

'Whatever you think I am, lady,' he cut in, cold anger underscoring his impatience now, 'I always pay my debts. So if you won't point out who——'

'Goddamn it to hell, will you folks look at that!' a man shrieked.

A chorus of voices was raised to confirm that many in the crowd had seen what shocked him. And the men in the human chain closest to the fire halted what they were doing.

Which caused many of those along the side street to yell angry demands to know the reason for the hold up. But few who saw what had been revealed by the collapse of the front wall were able to respond immediately to the questions. And many of those down the line surged forward to see for themselves: stare at the cause of the mass horror which was much clearer to see now that the smoke and flames thrown up by the fallen timber had diminished.

The interior walls of the building had been blasted by the explosion or burned down before the front one collapsed. So the wide-eyed crowd could see by the leaping light of flames across what had been the front office of the *Winton Examiner* into the pressroom at the rear. Where the printing press and other items of metal machinery had been sooted by smoke, maybe warped a little by intense heat, but remained largely intact.

One such piece of equipment was a gantry probably used for shifting heavy piles of newsprint from the delivery entrance at the rear of the building to the press. Now, starkly illuminated by the fires burning less fiercely on all sides, there hung from the centre by the neck in a noose the blackened head, arms and upper torso of a body.

Perhaps he had died by hanging before the blast exploded directly beneath him and disintegrated his legs and lower body. But probably not. It was more likely the noose of strands of wire was symbolic. In the same way as the hanging rope on the oak tree at Timber Bluff and the two miniature versions attached to the corpses of Judge Benedict and Warner McCormack: potent messages to ensure everyone knew the reason why the men had been killed.

'It's one of the O'Hara brothers!' Mary Henderson gasped, pressed a hand to her mouth as if physically to push down the nausea that abruptly threatened. And she wrenched her head forcefully to the side to avert her eyes from the grisly sight of the fire-charred nakedness of the hanging half man.

Then she swayed, forgot her ill-feelings for Edge as she clasped his arm tightly to keep herself from falling while she teetered on the brink of a faint.

All around them, other woman and many men were

likewise almost sick to their stomachs by the scene as rasping whispers began to be exchanged.

'Which brother you reckon it is?'

'Jack's a head taller than Edward.'

'I'd say that looks more like Edward, but I can't look at what's left of him no more.'

'Gotta be Eddy O'Hara. Jack and my man went off huntin' this mornin' for a couple of days.'

'Fletcher Grady again, gotta be!'

'Yeah. He must've gone outta his head after he heard that news from San Francisco.'

'Nah, it can't be. I heard Grady's locked up in a cell out back of the law office.'

'That's old news. Sheriff had him in the office, asked him a mess of questions was all. Then turned him loose.'

'That was a damn crazy thing for Nick Kenyon to do, seems to me!'

'We can all be wise after the event!'

The lawman had not been immune from the paralysing effect of the grisly sight revealed by the tumbling wall. And he was not among the first to recover from the shock. But his voice rang out loudest above the buzz of conjecture and accusation among the crowd:

'All right, you men! We all seen it now! That's enough gawping! Let's get this fire put out before it sets the rest of the town alight!'

He snatched up a nearby bucket and hurled it at the flames. And within a few seconds the human chain had reformed, was working as efficiently as before. The men spurred on by the undeniable possibility that other fires could start up. For each time another section of the building collapsed, the burning rubble exploded a shower of sparks that flew high to be carried by their own momentum through the billowing clouds of smoke, then drifted down on to the roofs of neighbouring buildings.

'First the judge and now Eddy O'Hara,' one of the old men who had been in the saloon growled sourly as the human chain attained its familiar rhythm. 'What's that crazy man plan to do? Kill off every last one of us on account of the mistake was made about Curly and that play-actin' girl?'

'That could be, Clem,' a woman told him in a doom-laden tone. 'But it's not only Judge Benedict and one of the O'Hara brothers are dead. Just before the explosion here, Kath Henderson found old man McCormack strangled in his bed at the hotel.'

'What?' The same monosyllable was voiced by many people as many more snapped their heads around to look at the woman who had made the revelation.

'That's Ernie O'Mally, the blacksmith, over there,' Mary Henderson said.

'And he wasn't just plain strangled and left like that,' the woman at the centre of attention went on, clearly enjoying her role. 'One of them crazy rope nooses like the one was on the judge was fixed to him, too!'

Mary Henderson had spoken with a tone of relief, like she welcomed the chance to cover her embarrassment with the mundane piece of information as she released her grip on Edge, stepped quickly away from him.

'Much obliged,' the half-breed said with a glance at the powerfully-built, middle-aged, sandy-haired man.

This as an over-endowed woman in a bright red dress squealed: 'Hell's bells!'

'What is it, Clarice?' O'Mally asked.

'Warner McCormack was on the jury, Ernie, that's the matter!'

'So?' somebody else demanded with angry impatience.

'Don't you see it? Benedict was the judge! The O'Hara brothers didn't make no secret of it in the newspaper that they reckoned the kid was guilty, oughta hang. And Warner was one of the jury brought in the verdict!'

'What are you saying, Mrs McIver?' Mary Henderson pressed. 'My father was also on the jury and——'

'Young lady, I'm sure glad I wasn't!' Clarice McIver countered raspingly. 'Or that I didn't go around bad-mouthin' the kid while the trial was bein' got ready. That's all I can say. Way it looks, Fletcher Grady figures to kill everyone that was against Curly!'

Mary Henderson swung toward Edge, looked about to

fasten a grip on his arm again. But she managed to keep herself from making any physical contact with him. She needed some kind of reassurance, though. 'Do you think that's what Mr Grady has in mind, Edge?' she asked nervously.

He told her flatly: 'Lady, if I could read minds, I'd start with women: find how come they keep changing them all the time.'

9

Just a handful of ghouls remained in the area of the burned newspaper building as the fire died down and the men who had carried Benedict's body out of the hotel earlier waited to take care of the mutilated corpse hanging from the gantry.

Those who stayed, silently waiting and watching, were ghouls because they were all either women or men too old to take a place in the human chain should the younger men become too exhausted to continue. Which was unlikely to happen, for with the dying down of the flames after the collapse of the final walls, there was little danger to neighbouring property and the former urgency went out of the firefighting.

The larger part of the crowd fragmented quickly in small groups. And as Edge moved off on his own he got the impression from a number of nervously suspicious expressions that those people who had been unconnected with the trial of John Grady took pains to stay clear of those who were. Like they were afraid they might be tarnished by association: or expected the killer to strike again at any moment and they could get hurt or worse in a backwash of new violence.

And soon, fear took a tight grip on everybody as the people overcame their shock at what had happened, reflected on what might take place now.

Doors were slammed closed, not primarily to keep out the cold. Drapes were drawn more tightly across windows. But chinks of light continued to gleam through the cracks in warped frames and between curtains: as people sat up in this early hour of a new day, talking about the terrifying implications of the series of violent events that had shaken the town.

Probably some people went straight back to bed, but felt the need to leave a lamp burning because of that primeval fear of the harmless dark, made worse when something frightening is known to have happened to somebody else.

Edge sensed the surrounding tension but was immune to its effects as he walked along River Road on the fringe of Winton's rundown area. Although it was just one of a dozen or so streets that cut off Travis, ran down to and bridged the Beaver, he guessed it was so called because it was the first of its kind when the town was established. Also, the way it twisted and turned and was narrow while all the other side streets were broader and arrow straight in a grid pattern added to the likelihood it was older than the rest.

Just a few of the buildings which flanked it were as old as the town: had stood there for long enough to be the reason for the road's existence all those years ago. Many others had gone up on both sides more recently: most of these business premises which were concentrated closer to the Travis Street end. Workshops rather than stores or offices. The houses were at the other end, more of them on the far side of the river than this side of the bridge.

O'Mally, who charged Edge a reasonable price for replacing two shoes on the roan, had told him Stan Craig lived at number forty-seven River Road. The blacksmith thought it probable Craig would still be up after the explosion woke his household. But he would not have come to take a look at the fire, or help to put it out, after he made sure it was not his livery that was being destroyed.

For, the blacksmith explained with a lack of understanding but no rancour, the liveryman carried keeping his nose out of other people's business to the extreme. He lived solely for his motherless brood of six children and his work which provided him with enough money to pay his way: just about.

The house was a large two-story ramshackle frame building beside the slow flowing river, icy looking in the moonlight. It had no front yard, but plenty of space on the river-side: an uncultivated, hard packed piece of ground that was littered with children's toys, most of them home made. A wooden rocking horse, a couple of swings fashioned out of iron pipe, rag dolls, a kiddy wagon with a wheel off, a drum, two wooden rifles and a doll's house.

A lamp burned in a downstairs room at the rear, its yellow light reaching to the blue glass panel in the door. Edge raised a fisted hand to knock on the door, but then held back when he heard a man singing. Softly and not well in the cadence of a lullaby.

Then he did knock and the singing was curtailed immediately, a door creaked, the level of light through the glass panel brightened, measured footfalls sounded, then a bolt slid and the front door opened to reveal the tall, thin, gaunt-faced man who had taken charge of the roan this morning. Tonight a moth-eaten robe was belted around his lanky frame, his hair was disarrayed and his eyes were dull from having his sleep disturbed. All of which made him look, perhaps, more disgruntled than he was to have a visitor so late.

He cradled a blonde-haired little girl of about five in his arms, the child sleeping peacefully with a hooked thumb sunk deep in her mouth.

'You wanna leave town right now, mister?' Craig asked without preamble, quiet but fast. And he hurried on before Edge could respond: 'If you'll just wait a minute while I bed down Agnes, I'll get you a key. You won't mind gettin' your horse outta the livery yourself, I hope? I don't wanna leave the kids here alone after they been scared outta their wits tonight.'

Edge waited patiently for the harassed and world-weary man to finish, then told him evenly: 'I came to pay what I owe, feller. Plan to leave before dawn, maybe. A key to the stable will be fine if you'll trust me. I'll leave it at the hotel for you?'

Craig nodded several times while the half-breed was speaking. Then muttered: 'I always trust people until they do somethin' to show they don't deserve it, mister. You wanna step inside? Like I said, wait while I put my youngest to bed?'

Edge could see into the dimly lit domestic scene beyond the front door. A hallway with several doors leading off. One at the rear open on to the kitchen where the lamp burned and some stove heat filtered out. Craig had been sitting in there, singing his daughter to sleep. This much of the house he could see looked cluttered with old and decrepit furniture. And the walls could do with a lick of paint. But it was at the extreme end of the scale from the neglected condition of the Oregon Trail Saloon. This house was comfortable, surely comforting to those who lived in it: a family that was complete unto itself, with no pride in personal possessions, need only of the essentials.

It looked to be the kind of house in which Edge could feel at ease: provided he had it to himself. He said:

'I'll wait out here, feller. Have a smoke, okay?'

'Whatever you want,' Craig answered with a shrug, turned and started up a creaking stairway to the right. He left the door open and Edge pulled it almost closed: to prevent his gaze from wandering inside rather than to keep the cold night air out of the stove-heated house.

He rolled the cigarette quickly, lit it with a match struck on the jutting butt of his holstered Colt. Hung it at the side of his mouth then once more pushed his cold hands deep into the pockets of the sheepskin coat. At no time did he regret the decision not to step inside the house, he convinced himself.

When Craig returned he had a padlock key which he gave Edge as he said: 'A buck and a half for tending the horse. Ernie O'Mally'll want——'

Edge cut in: 'I already paid him. He told me where to find you. We were both at the fire.'

Craig uttered a disgruntled sound as he closed his hand around the dollar bill and loose change Edge had given him. He didn't count the money, growled: 'I don't wanna hear about no fire, mister. If it's all the same to you. I got more than enough problems of my own raising a half dozen kids since Hannah passed on. Without takin' on other folks worries. But I'll hear all about it soon enough, anyway. Can't help pickin' up the gossip in a town like this is.'

He shook his head ruefully, then parted his thin lips in something close to a fleeting smile as he added: 'It's been a real pleasure doin' business with you, mister. You got a fine horse you take care of real well. I'll pick up the key from one of the Henderson family tomorrow like you say.'

Without knowing why he should be concerned, unless it

94

was on account of the little girl he had seen and the other children he had not, Edge asked: 'You serve on the jury at the John Grady trial, Craig?'

The liveryman had started to close the door. Now he paused abruptly, an embittered grimace replacing the near smile as he snarled: 'No, I didn't! And I thank folks to mind their own business the same way I mind mine. Goodnight to you, mister!'

He remembered his sleeping children in time to keep from slamming the door. And as Edge turned and stepped down off the stoop he felt doubly pleased he had not gone inside the house which would have started him to think seriously, perhaps, that there could be some place like it for him. But if there was, would he end up as soured toward his fellow men as——

He ended this line of thought with a rasped curse, removed the cigarette from his mouth so he could spit, fitted it back again. And acknowledged he was pretty much like the irascible Stan Craig already: he just didn't have the liveryman's finishing touches of family responsibilities.

The chill of the night air had masked the acrid taint of old burning by the time he moved unhurriedly back along the twists and turns of River Road, where glints of light continued to show here and there. But the only sounds he heard were of his own unobtrusive footfalls on the hard-packed street which had no sidewalks, the diminishing trickling of the Beaver River behind him and the far off howling of a couple of coyotes eager to satisfy some kind of hunger. For food, or companionship? Or a mate? Or a different kind of life.

'Edge! That's your name, isn't it?'

He was convinced for stretched seconds that the softly calling voice of the woman was in his mind. An illusion created because he was pondering his state of complacent satisfaction with so much that had happened for his good in this town. He was well fed, adequately rested, supplied with what he needed for the trail and his horse had been taken care of. He had enjoyed the willingly given body of a woman and had seen glimpses of the kind of life he wanted to lead: maybe.

If the compromises he needed to make were not too demanding!

'I sure could use a man like you, honest I could, mister!'

Edge stopped in mid-stride, knowing the woman's voice was not a figment of his imagination. He saw he was not far from the intersection of River Road with Travis Street. On one side was a single story red brick building with a display window flanking its double doorway. In one of these windows was an ornate looking funeral casket and in the other three designs of white stone grave markers. A sign stretching from one side of the building's roof to the other was painted: *Behan's Undertaking: Interments and Monuments*. On the other side a pair of gates in a ten-feet-high fence were cracked open under an arch that carried a sign proclaiming this was the entrance to *Grice's Wagon Repair Company*.

One of the gates was dragged open to widen the crack to a couple of feet as Edge angled in that direction. And then this gap was filled by a woman who pushed herself through sideways, out of the shadows into the moonlight. A woman, with garish blonde hair, bulkily built woman and heavily painted and powdered, with a black cloak draped over her shoulders. The cloak, tied at her throat, fell only to her waist: left an open inverted vee to show she wore a form-contouring white silk dress.

'No thanks, ma'am,' Edge said.

'What?' Her unlovely, overly fleshed face was made less attractive by a confused, slightly shrewish frown that masked her earlier expression of . . .

He suddenly realised he had not seen her face until that moment: had assumed she was flashing the age-old false smile of sensual invitation as a façade for avarice that women in her line of work developed. He said:

'I've seen your kind look worse, I guess. But never did see a lousier crib.'

'What? Oh, no! Please, mister!' She blurted the denial and the plea in a tense voice that was almost a squeal. Shook her head violently. 'This isn't what you think. God, no! I'm no whore trying to sell you a—My name's Roxanne Graham! I think there's a chance I'm going to be lynched tonight if

96

certain people get their hands on me!'

'That's friggin right, you murdering bitch!' a man roared from across the street. Punctuated the threat with a rifle shot.

The bullet blasted a long splinter of wood out of one of the gates, six inches from her head. Which, Edge realised as he snapped his own head around, got a bearing on where the rifleman was positioned, meant it had missed him by just a couple of inches at most.

A wisp of drifting grey smoke showed the shot was fired from between the cracked-open glass-panelled double doors of Frank Behan's funeral parlour. Then the rifle exploded a second time, the muzzle flash and spurt of smoke confirming that this was where the bushwhacker was hidden.

Roxanne Graham screamed and scuttled back behind the gates, both of which now showed a light-coloured scar against the dark, weathered texture of the timber.

And the gates slammed closed with a sound like the echo of the shot: covered the snarled curse that ripped from between Edge's pursed lips as he whirled, drew the Frontier Colt, thumbed back the hammer and levelled the gun from his hip as he dropped into the gunfighter's crouch.

'I'm going to give you a warn——' he started to drawl.

The man concealed behind the cracked-open doors of the building across the street interrupted him: '*You* I aimed to miss, mister!'

The half-breed's lips thinned and drew back to expose a narrow line of his teeth. And his eyelids drooped until a narrower glitter of ice blue left his eyes just a fraction from being tightly closed. He responded evenly: 'That you're still alive shows I've given you the benefit of the doubt on that, feller. But you better hear me out. I——'

'No, you shut up and listen!' he snarled, breathless with high anger. 'You don't make yourself scarce, I'll figure you plan to help that woman! After she slaughtered my brother and roasted him the way she did! Is that what you're doing, mister? Helping somebody who'd do something as disgusting as that?'

'I didn't!' Roxanne Graham squealed, then uttered a sob of terror.

'Jack ain't just makin' noises with his mouth, let me tell

you, mister.' This warning was spoken from the same side of the street as the wagon repair yard. A little way off to Edge's left, and behind him. 'I been huntin' with him lotsa times and I promise you he can hole you plumb between the eyes where you're standin' now if he wants.'

Edge turned just his head to look to where the second man stepped out of the alley between Grice's premises and the next door warehouse. And as he saw the short and fat man, fur-coated and hatted with a rifle canted to his shoulder, he recalled a woman at the scene of the explosion and fire had announced that her husband and Jack O'Hara were away from town on a two day hunting trip.

Roxanne Graham caught her breath, then sobbed again: immediately on the other side of one of the pair of bullet-scarred gates, like she was pressed tight against the timber.

The half-breed asked: 'You and O'Hara are pretty good buddies, I guess?'

'What?' The monosyllable was tremulous as the man found his wide eyes trapped by the ice cold, glinting gaze of the half-breed.

'I said I guess you and——'

'What's all the frigging talk, Alvin?' O'Hara demanded. 'We're here to take care of that murdering Graham woman, not——'

'He ain't makin' no sense to me, Jack!' Alvin broke in, his fear expanding by the moment as he found he could not wrench his gaze away from the unblinking, slit-eyed stare of the implacable half-breed. 'But I... I sure figure we oughta try to understand a guy like he is, Jack!'

'You understand me, stranger!' O'Hara snarled. 'And you do like I say, or I'll shoot you down like you're vermin!'

Edge muttered: 'Well, I tried to tell him.'

Then he turned his head around slowly to look back the way his Colt was aimed. Heard Alvin gasp like the man knew what was going to happen before the half-breed's forefinger moved against the trigger, the revolver in his rock-steady grip exploded a shot across the street.

A glass panel in one of the doors of the funeral parlour shattered.

O'Hara yelled in pain or maybe just alarm, started to snarl: 'You sonofa——'

Edge figured he had the time to swing his head and his gun hand toward Alvin. Which caused the man to freeze, his rifle midway down from his shoulder, free hand coming up to grasp the barrel so the Winchester would be level, maybe steady, from his hip.

'He the sort of buddy you're ready to die for, feller?' the half-breed rasped. Paused a moment, added: 'Let go of it or quit living!'

'I don't want to have to kill you, mister!' Jack O'Hara yelled, a shrill note of anguished frustration in his voice now. But there was resolute determination to do what had to be done as he wrenched open both doors.

Edge heard them bang against the walls at either side of the funeral parlour entrance, then the crash of shattering glass as shards of the already broken panel were dislodged and fell to the floor inside.

Alvin snatched a glance across the street, then did more than the half-breed had asked. Did not merely release his hold on the rifle so it could drop to the ground at the alley mouth: instead threw it forcefully away, so it hit the street heavily, far out of reach. He yelled as he dragged his imploring gaze back to Edge: 'No, Jack! He'll kill me! I know he will!'

'No I won't, feller,' Edge told him evenly.

'I don't want to have to kill you either, O'Hara!' a third man assured.

He was in the building behind the newspaperman. And Edge thought his voice was vaguely familiar as he directed a curt nod to acknowledgement of Alvin's confused look, then moved his head and Colt back toward the undertaker's premises.

'Fletcher?' Roxanne Graham rasped, the name sounding as little more than an exhalation of breath from just beyond the double gateway.

She began to ease open one of the gates again as, off to the side, Alvin vented a sound of dismay.

Edge spared the man a glance, was in time to see him start

to thrust his arms high in the air. Then bring one back down fast. In a gesture that could have meant he was going for a revolver inside his fur coat. But as Edge made to swing the Colt, Alvin uttered a choked scream, pushed his hand high alongside the other one and thudded down on to his knees. Tears squeezed from his eyes and coursed across his cheeks as he managed to force out of his constricted throat:

'Honest, mister, it's my damn weak stomach! I have to go——'

'Fletcher, is that really you?' the woman shrieked incredulously from a couple of feet behind Edge, no solid timber gate between them now.

'O'Hara, I'm warnin' you, don't——' Fletcher Grady began to snarl from somewhere close behind the other man in the funeral parlour.

But he was cut off in mid-sentence by a third rifle shot. With its accompanying muzzle flash and spurt of smoke. Along with a bellow of boundless rage this time.

The gates slammed shut behind Edge.

Jack O'Hara plunged out of the doorway between the windows displaying funeral artefacts: his hands working the lever action of his repeater. He was six feet tall and beanpole thin, dressed as warmly in fur clothing as Alvin. The Winchester was levelled from his left shoulder.

Edge fired the Colt as the rifle bullet ricocheted off the rusted metal latch at the centre of the gates.

Roxanne yelled her fear.

Jack O'Hara was pulled up abruptly in his tracks by the .45 calibre bullet sinking deep into his chest. But he was not dead on his feet: had the power of will and the physical strength to complete levering a fresh round into the breech of his Winchester in the wake of the spent cartridge case.

The rifle muzzle wavered, but then the man with a bullet in his chest drew a steady bead on Edge. Who thumbed back the Colt hammer, was a split second away from blasting a killing shot into the second O'Hara brother. As the man vented an animalistic wail of desperation: realised he was going to die and knew he had failed to end the life of his brother's brutal murderer.

But Edge stayed his finger at first pressure on the revolver trigger. Tracked the jerky progress of Jack O'Hara as a fusillade of gunshots crackled and the newspaperman was forced into a short forward run, the rifle dipping toward the ground, then slipping from his shaking hands a moment before the life drained out of him with the blood from the four gaping exit wounds in his chest. And he pitched full length to the ground, both arms stretched to their limit, hands clawed like he sought in the final second of his life to reach all the way across the street: drag Edge aside, wrench open the gates and take a throttling grip on Roxanne Graham.

An ominous, brittle silence descended over the scene of the brief gunbattle. The kind of silence that exists while people wait in awe for some new kind of interruption to bring them pain and grief.

No questions were spoken loud enough to carry outside the houses and along the streets of Winton. No doors crashed open. No footfalls thudded floorboards and hard-packed ground. So perhaps there were no questions asked in the silent darkness of households brought violently awake by the hail of gunfire. Perhaps the local citizens of this fine Oregon town had no desire to know what new terror had been unleashed on the community that had already been the scene of so much catastrophy in such a short period of time.

Then Alvin groaned, sank lower on his knees and brought down his hands. Clutched at his stomach as it growled and gurgled in turmoil.

And one pair of running footfalls was heard as a man came along Travis Street, rounded the corner on to River Road.

A gate of the wagon repair yard creaked open again and Roxanne Graham uttered a choked sound that was part sob, part a word nobody could comprehend.

'You get hit, woman?' Fletcher Grady asked, his taut voice pitched low as he emerged from the doorway of the funeral parlour, a Winchester canted across the front of his rangy body in a two-handed grip.

Maybe he saw her shake her head, or it was enough she remained on her feet, standing without swaying between the impassive Edge with the Colt in his hand and the kneeling Alvin who was clutching his stomach with both clawed hands, his face contorted by a grimace of desperate distress. Whatever, the tall and thin man with a gauntly angular face, wearing a long duster and no hat, halted close to where the prone, limply inert corpse of Jack O'Hara lay, accused the dead man with pained ruefulness:

'You stupid bastard, you forced me to do it.' He looked up, told the three people on the other side of the street: 'I never killed anything before. Even an animal or a bird, you know what I mean?'

Then, along with Edge, Roxanne Graham and Alvin, he turned to look toward the River Road intersection with Travis Street as Nicholas Kenyon came striding around a curve, right hand draped over the butt of the Colt jutting from his holster below the too-tight suit jacket.

The lawman pulled up short, slowly moved only his head to sweep his suspicion-filled eyes over the scene for several stretched seconds. Then he started cautiously forward again, his hand fisted tightly around the revolver butt now, his head steady but his eyes flicking back and forth along the full extent of their sockets. From twenty feet away, he said with harsh-toned menace:

'I want you men to drop your guns.'

'Oh no, it's happenin'!' Alvin groaned. And his stomach gave off a whole series of gaseous sounds as the frosty night air turned rancid with an unmistakable stink.

'Alvin Ridler, you should be ashamed!' Roxanne Graham accused sneeringly. 'A full grown man like you, not able to control himself that way!'

'I couldn't help myself, Mrs Graham,' the hapless man moaned, shifted his desperate gaze from her to Edge, to Grady and then the lawman. Who had not waited for his order to be obeyed, dropped the hand away from his own gun as he went to the bullet shattered O'Hara. 'I was so sure I was gonna meet my maker, I just . . . I been sick like this anyway. It's the reason——'

Shame, or the stink of himself, threatened him with nausea and he brought up a hand from his stomach to press it over his mouth.

Roxanne Graham squeezed her nostrils closed between a thumb and forefinger as she protested disdainfully: 'I figured I was pretty damn close to death's door myself, but I didn't——'

Edge had upended his Colt, now thumbed aside the loading gate, rotated the cylinder to let the spent cartridge slide out and fall to the ground. He interrupted the harsh-spoken woman, his own voice mild toned: 'Being close to death affects different people in different ways, ma'am.'

'I guess so, but a grown man oughta——'

The half-breed took a fresh round from a loop on his gunbelt, pointed it toward the kneeling man and showed a sardonic grin as he said: 'For him it was a moving experience.'

10

Winton remained a locked-up town, minding its own business as its lawman set about doing what it was necessary to do in the wake of the latest deadly violence to shatter the peace of the community.

Plainly the gunfire must have been heard all over town, but nobody was going to be the first to come out on to the streets to discover the cause of the gunbattle on River Road, to find who had participated in the exchange of fire, and its outcome.

So it was like every citizen had suddenly decided to adopt Stan Craig's philosophy: persuaded to this view by fear of the consequences of interference rather than any unselfish desire not to get involved in bad business that was none of their concern.

Those who were the participants welcomed being ignored in a situation which normally would have made them the centre of morbid attention.

This was particularly so for Kenyon, who had the lawman's innate aversion to people who hampered him in his peace-keeping duties by indulging their ghoulish curiosity after a tragedy: and his initial impulse to anger at the death of yet another Winton citizen was quickly controlled when he realised there was to be no gathering of bloodthirsty rubber-necks.

He even requested, rather than ordered, the three survivors of the gunfight to go to the law office and wait for him. While he arranged for Frank Behan to have his men take care of the new corpse: carry it back inside the funeral parlour where Jack O'Hara had unwittingly waited in such an appropriate place for his untimely end.

Alvin Ridler was granted speedy permission to make a detour by his house to change into clean, sweet-smelling clothing.

Fletcher Grady and Edge were allowed to keep their weapons, maybe because Kenyon realised he would be given an unwinnable argument by the half-breed if he made an issue of demanding their surrender.

Heading for the law office, Grady walked beside Roxanne Graham, the two of them huddled close together, talking in rasping whispers. And Edge followed several paces behind, rolled and smoked a cigarette, as the rangy man attempted to taunt the bulky woman into a quarrel. While she tried to placate his ruffled feelings with defensive explanations he refused to listen to.

It was no hardship for the half-breed to ignore them as he relished the intriguing lack of interest shown in him as he moved through the night-time streets of a small town after a fatal gunbattle in which he had taken a hand. Usually in such a circumstance, eyes would have tracked his progress, blatantly accusing him of being responsible for the violence: or he would have sensed surreptitious watchers peering at him with hostile contempt from the darkness behind moving curtains or cracked-open doors.

But the only ill feeling discernible in the terrified town tonight was between Fletcher Grady and Roxanne Graham, as the man continued to scorn the woman's efforts to convince him there was no reason to be mad at her.

Although he did not try to hear what was said as he trailed the couple off River Road, right on to Travis, across the street, then left at the intersection on to the eastern stretch of Juniper, the occasional rise in the level of their anger meant isolated words or disjointed phrases sometimes rang out louder than a whisper.

Ed O'Hara... love... explosion... truth... wits' end... could've been lynched... happened by... would I... how could I—

Travis was as quietly empty as River Road had been: Juniper the same.

The coyotes started to howl again in the distant west.

Kenyon's footfalls rapped on a run of sidewalk, but not for long.

Grady and Roxanne chose to keep to the hard-packed street rather than step up on to runs of hollow sidewalks. And Edge followed their lead, smoking the cigarette, his contentment with all that had happened since he arrived in this town increasing as he easily suppressed an impulse to anger with the woman for getting him involved in a shooting that was none of his concern. For of far greater importance was the total lack of interest in him by a whole townful of people: which was yet another example of something good achieved in Winton.

So Roxanne Graham had set in motion a circumstance that had seemed to come out of the kind of past he had decided he must seek: when frontier towns did not have ideas above their lowly stations, did not pretend they were something like eastern cities so the people who lived in them had to adopt citified ways and codes.

At the law office, Edge exchanged brief words with the still mad at each other couple, who were happy to have him wait outside, finish his smoke. They wasted no time in getting inside out of the frosty, breath-misting cold and through the window Edge saw Grady light a lamp on the uncluttered desk, then stoke some more heat out of the stove. This while the woman sat in the only chair before Kenyon's desk, wrapped the cloak tightly about her fleshy form and huddled down, elbows on the chair arms, her three-decker chin rested on clenched fists.

They called a halt to their quarrel until Grady completed these chores. Then, as he began to pace the floor of the spartanly furnished office, they recommenced their rasping disagreement. Went over exactly the same ground as before from the occasional word or phrase that reached outside to Edge.

It was just a few minutes before Kenyon swung around the corner of Travis on to Juniper, advanced along the centre of the street, head shifting from left to right with slow deliberation as he walked with a faintly rigid gait: in an attitude that suggested he was challenging any of his fellow citizens to dare to come out of the flanking buildings, or even call a question to him: break the spell the new killing had cast over the town.

But then he saw Edge, suddenly moved at a faster pace, his tough grimace replaced by a frown of petulant irritation. Which was matched by the tone of his voice when he snapped:

'I said for you to wait inside the law office, mister!'

Edge made a hook of the thumb of the hand with which he tossed away the dead cigarette butt, jerked it over a shoulder at the closed doorway, answered: 'I've already had enough trouble in Winton, Sheriff. I don't need to referee a lovers' quarrel.' He hardened his tone to add: 'And what the hell difference does it make where I wait?'

The exhange had brought a sudden end to the slanging match in the office. And after listening to the silence for a moment, Kenyon pulled a face, growled:

'Okay, okay. But get in there now and let's try to get this mess straightened out before anything else bad happens.'

The half-breed trailed the sheriff into his office. Kenyon said nothing, but from the sullen expressions on the faces of Grady and Roxanne he obviously shared a glower between them as he went to his desk, dropped into the chair behind it. Then, after he took off his hat and slapped it down on the desk, he generated a hostile frown to direct at Edge who was leaning against the wall beside the open doorway.

'Something, Sheriff?'

'I know you're a cold-hearted bastard, mister, but some of us have got blood in our veins, so shut the friggin' door, uh?'

'Could we watch our language in the presence of a lady, Mr Kenyon?' Fletcher Grady asked.

Kenyon abandoned his sneer at the half-breed, switched to an attitude of weary resignation as he heard footfalls out on the street, realised Edge had left the door open for Alvin Ridler. And he waited for the fifty-year-old, pale faced, too bright eyed and jug eared man, to step into the office and close the door before he responded to what Grady said.

'Everyone here except for Edge knows me pretty well. Should be able to figure I'm not myself after a day like it's been. Sometimes I take the trouble to act what I'm not, but... Hell, if Mrs Graham's a lady in anything except for being a female, I'm the next President of these United States.'

Grady vented a deep-throated sound, took a firmer grip on his rifle and made to step away from the wall beside the stove. But curbed the impulse to anger, stayed where he was when Roxanne rasped:

'It's all right, Fletcher!'

The lawman seemed a little disappointed that the heat was taken out of the situation. Then he sighed, shook his head, said in a sour-toned voice: 'Fine. So let's not stand on ceremony, horse around in any way: get this mess squared away soon as we can, uh?'

Alvin Ridler had been peering anxiously around, with the look of a trapped animal in his eyes: that were too bright, Edge decided, because of the snort of liquor he had taken while he was cleaning himself up. Now, even after he had seen nobody showed the slightest interest in him, he felt the pressing need to fill the silence that greeted Kenyon's words. He said nervously:

'I came as fast as I could, Sheriff. I'm so sorry for what happened. I just don't know how I'm ever gonna hold up my head in this town again.'

'You were afraid, Mr Ridler,' Kenyon allowed flatly, massaged his temples with the fingertips of both hands. 'And accidents happen. Jack O'Hara won't be doing anything in this town ever again. Except for getting buried. And what happened to him was no accident. Tell me about it, uh?'

Before the somewhat placated man could do as he was asked, the woman directed a withering glower at him, which seemed to have the physical power to press him against the wall across the doorway from Edge. She said tautly:

'They were going to lynch me, I know it!'

'Mrs Graham, I'll get to you in awhile,' Kenyon told her, then cocked his head to one side in a listening attitude.

The others did the same and Edge reached to the side, turned the knob to open the door a few inches: so it was clearer to hear the distant thud of hooves as two horses moved slowly along the far end of Juniper Street.

'Sounds like people leavin' town, headin' west,' Grady muttered as the sound of the hooves diminished.

Edge closed the door.

Roxanne blurted excitedly: 'The ones who're doing all the killing, maybe? You oughta get after them, Sheriff!'

'Be quiet, Mrs Graham,' Kenyon told her, 'before I forget I said I'd treat you like the lady you're not. Okay, Mr Ridler, get it told.'

Ridler, now garbed in a neck to ankle duster of lighter colour and later origin than that of Fletcher Grady, nodded vigorously. It even seemed he came close to flashing a smile of relief that talk promised to confine embarrassing memories to the back of his mind. But as all eyes became focused on him, he found it impossible to smile. And he had to make further excuse for himself.

'Yeah, well... Jack and me: we been out hunting way up near Beaver Lake, you know? But I got hit by this stomach bug, Mr Kenyon. Just about everything I ate went straight on through me and ... Well, it didn't only make huntin' well nigh useless, it was pretty damn draining, too, I can tell you. So, Jack and me, we decided to come on back home.'

He began to talk more quickly when the lawman pulled a face and uttered small sounds of disgruntlement at talk of the man's medical problems. 'We saw the fire from way off. And the closer we rode to town, the plainer it was to us it was the newspaper building was blazing. And Jack, he galloped on ahead. Me, I had to stop: take care of my churning guts.

'So I was way behind and the fire was near enough out when I rode in. Jack was waiting for me at Delmar Crocker's corral. Both of us have our horses took care of by Delmar when we don't have need of them.'

'You can leave out stuff like that, Mr Ridler,' Kenyon said, working his fingertips on his temples again: looking closer to exhaustion than anyone else in the office.

'Sure. Okay. Jack was in a hell of a state. Shook up real bad and wild animal mad. He told me about his brother getting killed in the fire at the *Examiner* building. Murdered for sure: how Ed was left strung up the way he was.'

'Yeah, we were there and we know that,' Kenyon said, his

voice tauter. 'Why did you and Jack O'Hara go gunning for Roxanne Graham?'

'Because Jack heard she was seen coming out of the *Examiner* building. Just a few minutes before the explosion that wrecked it and killed Ed, Mr Kenyon.' He gave the answer with conviction, but he was unable to hold the accusing gaze of the woman as she turned her head toward him.

'Listen, I can——' she began as she returned her gaze to the lawman across the desk.

'Later,' he told her with a dismissive hand gesture, nodded for Ridler to go on.

Dull eyed now, no longer drawing any Dutch courage from whatever he had gulped down, the sick-looking man sought to excuse himself to the glowering blonde, who was not so huddled up in her cloak now the stoked up heat of the stove was beginning to make an impression on the night air in the law office. 'Mrs Graham, I'm only saying what Jack told me.'

'O'Hara say who told him that?' Fletcher Grady growled from where he continued to stand rigidly near the stove, the rifle in a double-handed grip across his lower belly.

Kenyon grimaced at him, but looked expectantly at Ridler for an answer to his question. Which was a shake of the head, then:

'He just said he heard it being talked about. In the crowd watching the fire. Nobody knew he could hear what was being said. Because he stayed out of sight. Didn't want no one to know he was back in town. Before he found Mrs Graham. He said I had to help find her, be a witness to her confession before he killed her.'

The woman gasped and a tremor went through her fleshy body.

Fletcher Grady uttered a small, strangled cry and took a knuckle-whitening grip around the frame and barrel of his Winchester.

Kenyon sucked in a deep breath and shook his head as he slowly let it out.

Edge recalled his notion about small frontier towns getting to be like big eastern cities. But acknowledged to himself that it was nothing new, in times of strife, for not every citizen of such stable communities to remain bound by the civilised ways and codes.

It was clear to all of them what had been in Jack O'Hara's mind: later events had made this obvious. But to hear Alvin Ridler rattle it out this way acted to underscore the dire seriousness of what had happened in Winton tonight.

Then Grady, still struggling to come to terms with the effects of blasting the fusillade of shots into the newspaperman, muttered: 'Jack O'Hara wasn't no killer. He must've been outta his head.'

'Probably drove crazy by seeing his brother's corpse all smashed up like it was,' Roxanne Graham murmured, suddenly in the grip of a deep, grieving sadness.

'So you saw the corpse of Edward O'Hara?' Kenyon asked sharply, no longer irritated that others had taken the initiative. 'I didn't see you anyplace near the fire?'

'I saw Ed at Frank Behan's mortuary,' she explained morosely, unperturbed at how the lawman thought he had caught her out in a lie. 'After all the noise and the running around was done, I went to Behan's place on River Road. I just had to see poor Ed.'

She turned her head to meet the pained gaze in the eyes of Fletcher Grady. Then everyone looked at Alvin Ridler again, when he nodded vigorously and hurried to get to the end of his account.

'We saw her when she came out of there, Mr Kenyon. Jack already knew she wasn't at home. Nor at Fletcher Grady's place. He'd been to both of them before I got back to town. He didn't know where else to look, so that's why he asked me to help him search for her. We hadn't got started long when he saw her come out of the funeral parlour. But she saw us, too. Must have guessed something of what Jack had in mind to do for her. And she ducked down an alley.'

'They scared me real bad,' Roxanne confirmed, and swallowed hard as she recalled her feelings on the dark street.

Ridler nodded, pressed on: 'Town was real quiet by then. Only other person on River Road was the stranger.'

He glanced at Edge, looked quickly away again, like he

read censure in the impassive profile of the taciturn half-breed. 'He headed on down toward the river, like somebody out for a stroll.'

'Edge'll tell later what he was doing there, Mr Ridler,' Kenyon said tautly.

'Yeah, okay. Well, we knew Mrs Graham couldn't move fast without kicking up a row, so we stalked her real quiet ourselves. And I guess there ain't no doubt about it: it would be her stretched out on a slab in the mortuary—instead of Jack, I mean—if the stranger hadn't happened by again when he did. Took a hand.'

'I wasn't out for no evening' stroll!' Fletcher Grady growled, moved the rifle slightly to remind everyone of his part in the shooting on River Road.

Edge said evenly: 'For the record, Sheriff, I took a hand as a matter of self defence. The woman was safe in cover and O'Hara was gunning for me when I put a bullet in him.'

'I just said!' Kenyon snapped, 'you'll tell your story later. And all of you should know, everything said in this office is for the record. If it's pertinent to the investigation of the murders that have been committed in this town today.'

Riddler nodded. 'Yeah, my wife told me just now about Judge Benedict and Warner McCormack were——'

'Reckon you're about done, Mr Ridler?'

'Yeah, that's about it, Sheriff. I reckon I can back up what Mr Edge says. Mrs Graham asked him for help when he came back along River Road and——'

'Yeah, you're done,' Kenyon broke in. 'Mrs Graham?'

She had withdrawn into a private world of deep thought, chins sunk down on to her chest and hands supporting her head at each side. She stayed like that, her mind filled with memories or dreads, until Kenyon sharpened his tone to capture her attention.

'Mrs Graham, you can tell your story now, uh?'

'Yes, I heard you,' she growled, brought up her head slowly, to look around the office, show her resolute expression to every man in the room. Then she concentrated on the one across the desk from her, admitted ruefully: 'All right, I ain't gonna deny it. I already told Fletcher I was at the newspaper building with Edward O'Hara tonight. Edward and me, well... We been... We've gotten to be real good friends since——'

'They been screwin' together ever since she got fed up with me bein' such a grouch!' Grady put in bitterly.

'Shut up,' Kenyon told him, not taking his avid gaze off Roxanne's round face with its flesh-squeezed eyes, bulbous cheeks and almost negroid lips.

She nodded her agreement with Grady's crudely spoken truth. 'I've been going with Edward O'Hara... that way, for awhile. Reason we got started doesn't matter here and now. Because Edward was such a straightlaced man, had a reputation to keep up in Winton, of course, he never came to my place. And I never went to his house.'

'Straightlaced, my...' Grady snarled softly. And this time just a censuring glare from the lawman was enough to silence him as he readied himself to launch into an attack on the character of a dead man.

Roxanne directed a half angry, half rueful glance at Grady before she continued: 'It was always at the newspaper building. At night, after his brother and the boy who works for them left. I was there tonight, like I said. But I didn't do nothing to start any fire, set off any explosion. I swear it. I was gone from the *Examiner* building ten minutes or more before it went up that way.'

She waited to be told by Kenyon he believed her. He said:

'Jack O'Hara claimed he heard people say they saw you scooting away from there after the fire started, Mrs Graham.'

She nodded and sighed, told him: 'Yes, the people who said that weren't making it up. I hung around, Sheriff. Thought about going back inside. To tell Edward I wanted to end it with him. See, Fletcher had started to get over what happened to Curly and——'

'I won't ever get over my boy bein' hung for somethin' he never done!' Grady growled sourly.

Kenyon said stiffly: 'What happened to John Grady isn't an issue here.' Then he cleared his throat, glanced with something close to compassion at Grady, added: 'Well, not directly it isn't.'

'Yes, all right,' the woman said absently. She shook her head like she was annoyed at herself. 'Anyway, like I said: why I started up with Edward doesn't matter. Nor why I wanted to finish with him. I'd meant to tell him right off when I went to see him. But I just couldn't bring myself to do that. After I was outside for awhile, though, I got up the courage and I was just going back into the newspaper building, to get it said, when the whole place exploded. And I might have been killed, let me tell you. The way glass and pieces of lumber were flying all over. But I swear I never had anything to do with starting that.'

'That's the second time you've sworn it, Mrs Graham,' Kenyon said. Waved a hand in the air to dismiss any more attempts to reiterate the denial. Then used the same hand to gesture toward Grady that it was his turn to have his say about the night's events that culminated in the River Road shoot out.

Now that there had been time for heated feelings to cool, some clear thinking to be undertaken, Grady seemed as embarrassed as Ridler had been. Plainly he was not used to being at the centre of attention, and he hung his head. Acted surprised to see he still gripped the rifle in both his work-gnarled hands. He leaned it against the wall at his side, dry-washed his empty hands as he mumbled:

'Ain't much to tell you that you ain't already heard, Sheriff.'

'Just tell it like you know it happened,' Kenyon prompted.

'Yeah, okay. I knew about the fire at the newspaper building. Heard it go up and went to take a look at what was happenin'. But I never hung around there when I seen how some folks was lookin' at me strange. Even heard some of them say how I oughta be locked up in the jailhouse. How there was sure to be more and worse trouble, long as I was on the loose. So I went on home. And was just gonna go to bed when Jack O'Hara come bustin' in my place. Real mad he was, wavin' his rifle around and yellin' he'd put a bullet in my head if I didn't tell him where Roxanne was. Scared the... hell outta me and no mistake.'

Grady was speaking more fluently now, hands at his sides,

head up so he could show his frank expression to everyone in the office. 'He wouldn't say why he wanted to find Roxanne. But it was plain he didn't mean her any good. So when he went outta my place, I went after him. Took my rifle...' He touched the stock of the Winchester with a booted foot. '...with me. Saw him meet up with Ridley at Crocker's Corral. And when they headed into town, I went after them.'

He paused, like he needed more encouragement than the silent attention of his audience. Kenyon nodded and assured him:

'You're doing fine.'

Grady swallowed hard. 'I didn't see no sign of Roxanne on River Road until the shootin' started. That was after I'd trailed Jack O'Hara into the back of Frank Behan's place. See, I'd seen it when they thought they were on to somethin' and split up. Ridley ducked into an alley across the street and O'Hara went into the funeral parlour.

'Heard him shout he was gonna kill her. Then the stranger, he stood up for Roxanne.' He shrugged his narrow shoulders. 'Or for himself, if that's the way he tells it. I just know that after he put a bullet into O'Hara with his sixshooter, he was still up on his feet. And getting ready to do some more shootin' of his own. It figured it he dropped the stranger, then him and Ridler wouldn't waste no time in puttin' pay to Roxanne. So I pumped him full of lead. From the back, which was the only place I could shoot him. First time I ever killed any livin' thing, Mr Kenyon. That's the honest truth.'

Ridler protested quickly: 'And I ain't never killed nothin' but game. I told Jack I'd help him find Mrs Graham. But I didn' say I'd use my——'

'Okay, okay,' Kenyon broke in wearily, massaged his temples again. 'I'll believe the both of you. Same as I'll believe Mrs Graham. For now. Until I find out different. Mrs Graham?'

'Sheriff?'

'While you were waiting around outside the *Examiner* building? After you left Ed O'Hara?'

'Yes, Sheriff?'

'Did you see anyone else around there? Or hear anything

that made you suspicious something was wrong?'

She shook her head, answered morosely: 'No, I didn't, Sheriff. I wish I did. So I could tell you who did that awful thing. Like I said, maybe whoever left town awhile ago?'

'Guesses won't get us anywhere,' Kenyon broke in. Then: 'How about you, Edge?'

'I'm with you, Sheriff,' the half-breed said evenly. 'After this town hung an innocent man, you need to be sure of the facts before——'

'I don't mean that, and you damn well know it!' Kenyon snarled. He reached out to the sides and gripped both corners of the desk. Held on like to let go would cause him to lose control of his temper, and spoke with studied evenness: 'I've got the picture of the part you played in the shooting, mister. Like to know now just what you were doing on River Road at the right time?'

'Seemed to me like it was the wrong time, Sheriff,' Edge told him. 'But I know what you mean. I called on the liveryman.'

'The liveryman?'

'Stan Craig. He lives at number forty-seven River Road, down on the bank of the Beaver.'

'Yeah, I know Craig's the liveryman and where he lives!' Kenyon growled.

Grady said tautly: 'You sayin' you planned on leavin' town right after what happened at the newspaper buildin', stranger?'

'The plan was made before tonight's trouble, feller,' Edge told him evenly, ignoring his implication. Then said to Kenyon as he dug out the key Craig had given him, held it up: 'Went to pay him what I owed for taking care of my horse. Got this so I can take my horse out of the stable and leave without troubling him if he's not up early enough.'

'I didn't mean nothin',' Grady muttered.

'Gee, I'm sorry, mister,' Roxanne said. She sounded genuinely contrite, her over-fleshed face showing an expression to match the tone. 'None of this is anything to do with you at all. But I was real desperate when I saw Jack O'Hara was trying to kill me. I just had to——'

116

Kenyon snorted his impatience, growled: 'Don't you worry none about Edge, Mrs Graham. He's the kind who can take care of himself.'

'It's what I like to do best,' Edge said.

Kenyon let go of the corners of his desk, sighed, said with resignation: 'If you want to get out of here—and out of this town—and start doing it, mister, that'll be fine with me.'

Edge straightened up from the wall, acknowledged: 'Much obliged, Sheriff.'

Kenyon shook his head. 'Don't thank me. Like Mrs Graham said, this is nothing to do with you. But if you want to feel grateful to somebody, let it be Roy Elrick. For changing his mind.'

'That so?'

'Had my way, you'd be in jail for cutting him up the way you did. But he got cold feet when it came to swearing out a complaint against you.' Kenyon scowled his contempt for the drummer's lack of courage, added wryly: 'Guess he thought it might turn out to be a fatal complaint: for him.'

Edge paused with the door partly open, letting a stream of frosty air into the stove warmed office, which caused Roxanne to wrap the cloak more tightly around her as Grady growled bitterly:

'Guess I know how you feel, Mr Edge: havin' folks think so bad of you. Saw what it did to my boy. And it's startin' to get to me now.'

As the door closed behind the half-breed, Alvin Ridler said: 'I don't honestly think a man like that ever cares much about what people think of him.'

Outside, Edge stiffened when he overheard this. Showed a thin-lipped, glittering-eye scowl as he turned to head for the hotel. Then he forced the expression to change into a grin as he muttered softly to himself: 'Right, Alvin. If I started to think otherwise, I'd be as full of crap as you used to be.'

11

Edge's plan to leave Winton before dawn on the trail to California did not work out. For when dawn broke he was still soundly asleep.

Mainly this was because he had gotten to bed so late. But another reason for waking so late in the new day was the unnatural quiet that was blanketed over the Oregon town that morning.

He became aware of this eerie silence the instant he snapped open his eyes: knew from the intense brightness of the light filling the room that the sun was far advanced on its climb up the south eastern sector of the sky. And since it was long past daybreak, the hotel should have been humming, if not buzzing, with activity and sound. Likewise, the streets: even in a backwater country town like Winton, they should have gotten started into some kind of bustling stride.

He had awakened as usual with total recall of all that had happened during the long day and half the night before he slid into this bed for the second time: on this occasion with the cold and hard wood and metal of a Winchester rifle for company beneath the covers instead of the warm and compliant body of Mary Henderson.

It took him only a second to estimate the approximate time of the new day: somewhere between eight and nine. Which had to mean there was something extraordinary about the hotel and the town being so quiet.

When he got out of bed he found the brightness of the sunlit room had no relevance to its warmth. He quickly pulled on his pants and shrugged into his shirt, then went to the window, moved aside the net curtain and gazed impassively down on to Travis Street.

Nothing moved within his restricted range of vision except for the darting shadow of a fast-flying bird. He opened the window and grimaced at the bite of the outside air that felt hardly above freezing point. Then he thrust his head and shoulders out, looked to left and right. Checked that the silent emptiness extended from the nearer southern end of Travis between the church and the cemetery to the far extremity of the street beyond the charred remains of the newspaper building.

It was like the dead of night, but lit by the brilliant sun instead of the glittering moon. A sun that was just warm enough to have melted the frost on areas where it reached: but patches in shadow were still as sparkling white as the snow on the far distant higher ridges of the Cascades on three sides of Winton.

But it was not sunlit night. Nor had some virulent disease struck down every inhabitant of the town while they slept. Neither had the three brutal killings that shattered the composure of Winton yesterday struck so much terror into the minds of the people that all of them had felt compelled to sneak away before the dawning of a new day which might threaten further violence.

Had they..?

He made another, slower survey of the scene. Shifted his unblinking gaze from the church, along a row of houses which stood back from the street behind neat front yards. Next the blacksmith forge of Ernie O'Mally, then some stores sharing a roofed sidewalk: one of these the meat market operated by Alvin Ridley. The impressive, granite-built courthouse, one of Winton's two banks, a couple of tidily-weeded vacant lots, the stage line depot, the telegraph office and a building he knew had two brass shingles on the wall beside the front door: which named the doctor and the dentist who lived and practised their professions on different floors of the big frame house.

Here he curtailed his study of the eastern side of Travis Street's southern stretch. He had already seen sign that if Winton was abandoned, some of the people had not left so long ago, for here and there smoke wisped from chimneys, given off by the dying embers of stove fires in need of tending. Now he saw for sure that somebody else remained in town, for a face showed at an upper story window of the house shared by the doctor and the dentist.

He reflected inconsequentially that he could not recall which shingle directed patients upstairs: whether it was likely to be the doctor or the dentist who was at the window. Certainly it was a man, peering unwaveringly through the closed window at the open one in the façade of the hotel: a man unconcerned he had been seen by the half-breed.

Edge shivered as he closed the window and let the curtain fall into place across it. He was so cold already it was no hardship to wash with the icy water poured from the pitcher into the bowl on the nightstand. But a cold water shave held no appeal and he had a notion the old-timer named Dan who supplied water for his hot bath yesterday would not be available in the silent hotel this morning.

He dressed fully for the weather outside, picked up his gear and left the room. Moved along the hallway between closed doors from behind which no sounds came. But some of the rooms were occupied, he was certain of this. He was not sufficiently intrigued by the situation to hammer on any door and demand to know what was happening in Winton this morning.

As he descended the elegant curve of the staircase the grandfather clock in the lobby began to chime. He was downstairs, close enough to see the face of the clock, before it completed striking the hour of nine.

He made the conscious effort not to resent events that had conspired to have him sleep in so late: because he was in no rush to get to California, it would be pointless. He was a little bothered that there was no aroma of coffee to get his taste buds working as he crossed the lobby. But he thought only fleetingly about the attraction of a cup of hot coffee: in much the same way he had contemplated a hot water shave. It would be welcome, provided he did not have to fix what was necessary himself.

He hefted his gear on to one shoulder and pushed out between the double doors. And now that he was fully dressed against the coldness of the bright morning air he felt a modicum of warmth in the sun on his face.

There was no longer a man at the upper story window of the building diagonally across the street as Edge swung to the right, headed for Stan Craig's livery stable across a wagon-wide alley from the hotel. The key that had led him into so much trouble last night turned smoothly in the padlock. The interior of the building was as neat and clean as the well preserved façade of the place promised.

His roan gelding was one of a dozen horses stalled in the livery and most of the animals reacted skittishly to the intrusion of the half-breed. But they quickly calmed as he took his mount out of the stall and saddled him with practised speed.

But it was an uneasy quietness that filled the horseflesh-reeking air. Like the one that had existed before he entered the livery, Edge thought: some unreasoning equine sense warning the animals there was something very wrong about the near utter silence clamped over the town. Like the total calm before a crashing storm.

The clop of the roan gelding's hooves sounded obtrusively loud when Edge led him out of the livery. He closed the double doors and left the key in the unfastened padlock. Swung up into the saddle and immediately felt the horse's urgent desire to gallop flat out away from the strange atmosphere that existed here.

But it was only an easy walk that Edge was about to command when he stayed his hands on the reins, turned in the saddle at the sound of an opening door that carried clearly across the hundred and fifty yards of intervening street.

'Like a word with you, Edge!' a man called from the stoop of the building with two brass shingles hung on the wall beside its doorway.

By way of acknowledgement, Edge wheeled his horse through a half turn. Saw the frame that went with the face from the window was frail-looking: the man no taller than five feet three inches and weighing little more than a hundred pounds. He was neatly attired in a dark blue suit, white shirt with a stiff collar and a bootlace tie. He carefully placed a grey derby on his grey-haired head as he stepped carefully down off the stoop and started across the street with a gait that suggested he was taking trouble not to kick up dust to soil the cuffs of his pants and dull the sheen of his highly polished shoes.

Edge thought he was the doctor rather than the dentist: he just did not look strong enough to pull teeth. And before he was halfway across the street, the half-breed revised his estimate of the man's age: from fifty some to close to seventy when he saw the crinkled texture of the freshly-shaved, purple-mottled skin.

When the diminutive man was closer still, it was possible to read the expression of contempt on his time-lined features. And the same degree of ill feeling sounded in his thin-toned voice when he said:

'I wish to state at the outset, sir, anyone capable of inflicting such wounds on the face of another rates low in my estimation.'

Edge pursed his lips, dug the makings from a shirt pocket under the skeepskin coat and reminded impassively: 'You said a word, feller. That's a whole bunch of them and what they all say doesn't amount to anything new to me.'

The man came to a halt fifteen feet away from where Edge sat the eager-to-leave gelding, modified the scowl to a faint sneer as he said curtly: 'I am Doctor Ralph McCloud.'

Edge replied as he started to make a cigarette: 'I don't figure I'm going to be pleased to meet you, Doc.'

McCloud stiffened, snapped: 'I dislike intensely being referred to as Doc, sir!'

Edge nodded almost imperceptibly. 'So you don't like my ways or my manner, Doc? You mind telling me what we're doing here wasting time?'

McCloud cleared his throat, like he had changed his mind at the very last moment about what he was going to say. Then said quickly: 'I'm given to understand you are an intelligent man who sometimes pretends to be obtuse, Mr Edge. It was just *my* manner of speaking when I mentioned a word: which I am sure you realised perfectly well. As for whether our time is being wasted, I am prepared to pay you for your's.'

'No you're not, Doc,' Edge countered.

'I beg your pardon?' He was insulted at being contradicted.

The half-breed struck a match on the stock of the Winchester jutting out of the forward hung boot, lit the cigarette before he explained evenly: 'My time's worthless to you. So if you pay me, it'll be for something you want me to do with my time.'

Now McCloud looked like he was either going to spit or vent a curse. Managed to suppress his irritation without resorting to either as he asked: 'Are you willing to listen to what I have to say, sir?'

Edge shrugged, answered: 'If talk's cheap, Doc, I figure listening has to be on sale. Let's find out if we can strike a bargain.'

12

Doctor Ralph McCloud shook his head, dug a hand into an inside pocket of his jacket and growled: 'Nicholas Kenyon was certainly right about how infuriating you can be, sir!'

His hand came out holding a case of cigars. He took one from the case and after he had bitten off the end had a valid excuse to spit. Which he did, with force.

'Some lawmen sometimes are right, Doc,' Edge told him as he stroked the neck of the horse, the gelding's mood of unease not helped by the hostile attitude of McCloud. 'Be obliged if you'd start to get to the point. My own time isn't worthless to me. Figured to trade it for some miles south this morning.'

'Will you be willing to delay your departure in exchange for a hundred dollars cash, Mr Edge?' the diminutive medical practitioner asked flatly, the brightness of the cloudless sky causing him to squint as he peered up at the mounted man.

'For what?'

'Prevent senseless killing, sir.'

'Winton has a sheriff who doesn't always get things wrong to take care of that kind of problem.'

'Nicholas is not in town this morning.'

'Along with a whole bunch of other people it looks like.'

'What?' McCloud had mastered the trick of striking a match on a thumbnail. He did it now, lit the cigar which may have tasted no better than it smelled from the less than contented expression that remained on his wrinkled face as he expelled a stream of smoke.

'I thought Winton had turned into a ghost town until I saw you at the window, Doc. Then got the idea that some of the hotel guests are keeping their heads down in their rooms.'

McCloud sucked in some more smoke, let it trickle out this time as he looked up and down the deserted street, nodded and said: 'Yes, I can see how that could seem to be so if you didn't see how this situation came about.'

'I didn't.'

'The town is far from empty, Mr Edge. I understand you were in the law office last night when Vernon Bassett and Helen Cannon left town?'

'I'm blaming my late start on it, Doc. Nobody knew who they were at the time.'

'That's who they were, Mr Edge. Vernon operates the wire service.' He gestured toward the telegraph office next door to the building he shared with the town dentist across the street. 'And Miss Cannon clerks at the stage line depot over yonder.'

'They weren't eloping, I guess?'

'What?' McCloud squinted up at Edge astride the roan gelding again. Grimaced and muttered: 'Oh, I assume you are being facetious?' He looked away so he could untangle the flesh around his eyes. 'In view of what happened last night—to the O'Hara brother at the *Examiner* building and to Warner McCormack and Judge Benedict—the sheriff felt it was his duty to go after them.'

He made a dimissive gesture with the hand holding the cigar, hurried on forcefully: 'Of course, it's ridiculous to give houseroom to any idea that Vernon and Miss Cannon could be responsible for such a dreadful series of crimes. But the timing of their departure was unfortunate. Nicholas had to assume the worst.'

'The worst is what lawmen always think of people, Doc,' Edge put in. 'They seem to figure it's part of their job.'

'I suppose we are all entitled to our own opinions!' McCloud snapped, then sighed and moderated his tone and expression. 'After what happened to the luckless Grady boy, Nicholas must give his father and the Widow Graham the benefit of every doubt.'

A fleeting grimace showed that in this matter his opinion differed from that of Winton's lawman. 'I understand you were present when they told Nicholas what they knew of how the O'Hara brothers met their untimely ends? And you, of course, had a direct involvement in the death of one of the brothers yourself?'

He directed only a squinting glance up at Edge now.

The half-breed said: 'The sheriff sounds like he does a lot of confiding in you, Doc?'

'What's that?' His thoughts had been diverted elsewhere: maybe in the direction of how much credence he gave to Edge's account of the way Jack O'Hara died in the gunbattle on River Road.

'Kenyon told you a lot, Doc. Late last night or early this morning.'

An emphatic nod. 'Yes, I see what you mean. Well, Winton's sheriff is required to keep me informed on such matters. I'm the mayor, Mr Edge. And Nicholas always makes a point of doing so. He stopped by to see me on his way out of town. Immediately after he discovered just who had ridden out in the night.'

'Okay, Doc.'

'What is?'

'Fine, so far. I see how come you know so much about what's going on. Now we get to what's worth a hundred bucks to you.'

'Not to me personally sir,' McCloud countered firmly. 'The money comes out of the community law and order fund. I hope to hire you as a deputy.'

Edge made a conscious effort to remain impassive as a façade for the surprise he felt at the revelation when he answered: 'You do?'

'I have the authority. You see, I am not just the mayor. I'm also a permanent deputy sheriff myself. Sworn to keep the peace whenever Nicholas is away. The only regular deputy Winton has.'

Edge wasted just a few moments on considering why the citizens of this Oregon town should have such a frail and elderly individual to hold the office of deputy sheriff. Decided it had to be little more than an honorary position: or maybe McCloud had started out with the job as a young man and gotten to be too firmly entrenched to be removed. He asked: 'Why do you want another now?'

'It won't be for the first time, sir. I have found it necessary to deputise other men on occasion in the past.'

'None of them work out?'

'What?'

'Why pick me this time?' Edge asked, moved his head in a token gesture of encompassing the deserted length of Travis Street, its emptiness seemingly stressed by the way the brilliant sun gleamed on so many polished surfaces. 'Unless the town isn't still filled with people like you say it is?'

'As far as I am aware, sir, only the sheriff and the two people he is trailing have left Winton since yesterday,' McCloud answered. 'So there are plenty of men in town, some of whom I have deputised in the past. But this is a unique situation and you're the only suitable man for the job today.'

'Sheriff Kenyon back your opinion, Doc?'

'Nicholas would doubtless disagree violently with my decision, Mr Edge. And I have to tell you that in normal circumstances I adhere strictly to my principles when I make moral judgments. I see nothing to choose between small and great wrongs if there are no extenuating circumstances to excuse the wrongdoer. But on this occasion I feel I must depart from my long and firmly held beliefs for the good of my fellow citizens.'

Edge allowed his thoughts to wander away from the frail-looking man standing beside his uneasy horse, the strangely empty street. To reflect on how he had acknowledged to himself he would have to make adjustments to long held beliefs of his own. If he were to find something close to what he wanted: now he knew what he truly had wanted all this time no longer existed.

'At this very moment, sir,' McCloud went on grimly, 'every man I would generally consider swearing in as a deputy is either cowering at home or is at the meeting hall.'

Now Edge did not attempt to conceal his response to what the doctor said. And McCloud showed a mirthless smile of satisfaction that he had triggered an intrigued reaction from the inscrutable half-breed. Then he replaced the cold smile with a scowl of contempt as he went on:

'Either refusing to make a stand one way or the other. Or working up the courage to commit the most despicable of crimes.'

'Kill somebody, you said.'

McCloud snorted, shook his head. 'I thought you were a stickler for words, sir? I said if I recall it accurately that I wanted to hire you to prevent senseless killing.'

Edge nodded. 'Yeah, you're right, that's what you said, Doc.'

'Quite. Two potential victims are involved, Mr Edge. And the precise manner of killing being contemplated is lynching. The illegal hanging of Fletcher Grady and Roxanne Graham.'

Ever since McCloud had said that many of the silent buildings along Travis Street were occupied, Edge had remained receptive to being watched. But not for the first time when he knew he could be under surveillance, he failed to detect any sign of it. And he guessed this was because there was no hostility in the minds of anyone who might be peering surreptitiously out on the bright, hushed street.

Or, perhaps, those Winton people who wanted no part of what was happening in their town this morning had withdrawn from it to such an extent that they did not even dare take a peek outside until they knew the decision had been taken one way or the other. One way, the deed had been done.

'Tell me something, Doc?'

'Provided it does not take too long, sir. There will be no urgency until those at the meeting hall have cast their vote for what I am convinced will be a misguided decision. But time is passing.'

Edge checked the impulse to say that McCloud's verbose manner of speaking ate up more time than was necessary to make his point. Instead, he asked: 'Just what do you figure to buy for a hundred bucks, Doc?'

McCloud sucked in smoke, let it explode out of his mouth and nostrils and formed his sparsely fleshed features into an expression that looked like a sneer in the making. But next did something with his thin and bloodless lips and got a gleam in his dark grey eyes to form a frown of determination before he answered: 'A man not afraid to make a stand against mob rule, sir. Albeit for a price. I am not afraid to make such a stand myself, from a sense of duty which I would not expect you to possess. But alone I would serve no useful purpose.

And who knows: if we're seen to be making such a stand, others may be shamed into ... persuaded to join us?'

Edge gave the offer and its explanation no more than fifteen stretched seconds consideration while McCloud smoked his cigar with quick and jerky movements of his hands and a series of rapidly changing expressions came and went across his face. He was plainly anxious to hear the half-breed's response but resigned to accepting whatever decision was made: knew there was nothing more he could say, maybe no amount he could add to the fee, that would make any difference.

'In advance, Doc?'

'What?' Another squint against the brilliantly blue sky behind the mounted man. 'Oh, the money? Certainly.'

He reached inside his jacket on the other side from where he kept the case of cigars. Drew out an envelope thin enough to show that few of the bills it contained were of small denomination. 'As mayor, I have access to the community funds. And Earl Caldwell, who runs the bank where the funds are held on deposit is not one of those moved to go to the meeting hall.'

He pushed the slim brown envelope up at the mounted man. But Edge kept both his hands occupied with the reins draped over the saddle horn when he said:

'There are a couple of conditions?'

McCloud looked perturbed, asked flatly: 'State them, sir.'

'There's no guarantee I can do what you want.'

'But you'll try your best, I'm sure?'

'I never accept money for less than full effort, Doc,' Edge told him.

'Quite.' He looked almost embarrassed.

'Second one: if I get them away from the lynch mob, I can only guarantee to keep Grady and the woman from being strung up if they leave town with me. You want to lock them up here in Winton, you'll have to see they're protected.'

'I feel sure that people in their situation will agree to anything necessary to stay alive, sir.'

'Where's the meeting hall?'

McCloud took the cigar out of his mouth, gestured with it

toward the intersection. 'Far western end of Juniper Street, across from Delmar Crocker's corral.'

'Grady and the woman?'

'At the meeting hall, Mr Edge.'

'So how do you know it hasn't happened yet?'

McCloud sucked in smoke, blew it out with a snort. 'I am old, but not yet senile, sir! I made absolutely sure of my facts before I made this approach to you.'

He seemed to be waiting for some kind of apology, scowled when he did not get one and went on: 'The deed, if it is to be done, will be perpetrated at the place where Edward O'Hara's mutilated corpse was seen to be hanging last night. Those engaged in the infamy that is to take place realise it will constitute a ghastly blemish on the fine record of Winton, its citizens past and present. What is left of the newspaper building will be razed to the ground and every last trace of it will be eradicated after the deed is done.'

'That's where I'll give it my best effort to stop the lynching, Doc,' Edge told him, took the envelope, put it in a pocket of his sheepskin coat.

'Not alone,' McCloud said. He dropped his quarter-smoked cigar, ground it out under a heel of a polished shoe as he reached into an outside pocket of his jacket. Produced two silver stars, pinned one to a coat lapel and held up the other toward Edge.

'I'm best at doing my best alone,' the half-breed drawled. 'By my own rules.'

McCloud shook his head emphatically, replied adamantly: 'I cannot condone fighting vigilante tactics with more of the same, sir. This matter must be handled in a right and proper manner: officially by rule of law.'

Edge held back for just a moment, then shrugged, accepted the badge and pinned it to his coat front on the left, asked: 'You got a gun, Doc?'

'No!' He was shocked by the notion of packing a firearm. 'I am a doctor first and foremost, a lawman second. My prime consideration is the saving of life rather than taking it.'

'I can't guarantee your life.'

'I place no such condition on you, sir. I do insist you resort to the use of a weapon only in the event that all else fails. Despite the utter madness that is happening here today, Winton is a civilised community. The law of the gun has not applied in this town in many years.'

'I'll do my best, Doc.'

'Consider yourself sworn in, Mr Edge.'

Edge pursed his lips, relit his cigarette which had gone out from inattention where it angled from the side of his mouth. On a stream of tobacco smoke growled: 'Sure, Doc. And you consider yourself cussed at.'

13

Edge heeled the gelding into a slow walk, moving in the opposite direction to the one he intended to take when he stepped out of the hotel this morning.

The old man stayed alongside the horse, no longer taking any trouble to stop the dust rising now the animal kicked up a small cloud with every step.

For the first time this strange morning, the half-breed felt eyes other than those of McCloud on him. But he did not seek to pinpoint the positions of any of the watching people: was still sure that no one in this area of town meant him ill will: yet. Maybe, on the contrary, having seen he had made some kind of deal with their doctor, mayor and deputy sheriff, they were even rooting for him.

But if this were so, the only support they offered was moral: Ralph McCloud's hoped-for help triggered by a sense of shame did not materialise.

There was no further talk between the two men until they had advanced across the intersection and both had peered along the western stretch of Juniper to the plank bridge spanning the Beaver River and beyond. Delmar Crocker's corral was in view at the far end on the left, but the meeting hall was obscured by the intervening bulk of the schoolhouse. Juniper Street was as eerily silent and empty as Travis.

'You don't think it would be better to confront them at the meeting hall, sir?' McCloud asked. 'Stop this madness before it starts?'

'It's already started, Doc,' Edge reminded the old man. 'What you want me to do is stop it ending the wrong way. If it turns out they decide to do the right thing, there's no point in stirring up more trouble.'

He looked down at McCloud, expected him to say something about a refund of the hundred dollar fee. But he merely nodded, showed a brief expression of faint hope in such an outcome. Then he glanced quickly to left and right, back over a shoulder: resurrected the expression of embittered disappointment that none of his fellow citizens had joined them.

That was the extent of talk until they had run the gauntlet of curious attention from detached observers and reached the malodorous, flame-charred wreckage of the *Winton Examiner* building. When McCloud vented a shocked, choked cry and gasped:

'Oh my God, look what they've done!'

As Edge surveyed the scene from where he had reined in the gelding on the centre of the street between the burnt out building and a row of small stores, it looked much the same as he remembered it from last night. Minus the grisly remains of Edward O'Hara strung up from the gantry in the former press room. Except that this morning, a pair of noosed ropes had been fixed to the gantry: one at either side of the steel cable with which O'Hara had been suspended. The sooted blackness of the cable emphasised the white newness of the ropes.

'Seems some people figure the result of what's happening in the meeting hall is a foregone conclusion, Doc,' Edge said as he swung down from the saddle.

'This is something I was not informed of,' McCloud said thickly, unable to tear his gaze away from the scene of destruction which was dominated by the ominous lengths of unmoving ropes.

The smell of old burning caused the already disturbed gelding further unease and Edge retained a firm hold on the bridle as he raked his narrow-eyed gaze all around. Eyes continued to peer at him and the old man, but without malevolence. The people who had fixed the new ropes to the gantry had not stayed here to guard the place of future executions.

None of the stores across from the burnt-out building were open. And the stoves beneath their chimneys were cold. But there were smoking chimneys and some sounds of normal daily life from the area of narrow streets spread out in back of the stores on Travis. A hum of subdued talk, the cries of babies, the barking of a dog. So it seemed most of the people who lived in the poorer quarter of Winton were endeavouring to remain unaffected by what was happening elsewhere. But they could not totally ignore it: they stayed off the main streets and there was a subdued quality about the sounds they made as they attempted to pretend everything was normal.

'Nobody from Old Town is involved, Mr Edge,' McCloud said. And directed a look of something akin to affection toward the section of Winton that took up the north west corner of the community. 'Mostly Indians or of Indian extraction. Many with French or British parentage. Keep themselves to themselves.'

There was a hitching rail outside a cafe beyond the sidewalk-fronted line of stores. The gelding was not happy to be hitched to the rail, but was well schooled enough to submit to Edge's wish with no stronger protest than a snort and a baleful look.

McCloud had remained standing on the centre of the street, watching what the half-breed did. But probably he did not see it as he devoted his mind to wishful thoughts about how much better it would be if everyone in Winton followed the example of the people of Old Town.

But he did not fail to note that the half-breed had slid the Winchester out of the boot on the saddle, sloped it to his shoulder when he turned away from the horse. He said, quickly and nervously: 'Oh, I sincerely hope you will have no need to use that, sir?'

Edge almost growled that it didn't matter too much one way or the other to him. But instead he made no acknowledgement to the worried man as he walked past him, then along what had been an alley between the McIver Drugstore and the newspaper building before one of the flanking walls collapsed in the fire. There was charred debris on the ground which sent up small clouds of powdery ash as the half-breed trampled it underfoot.

McCloud trailed him, deeply frowning, unconcerned

about the neatness of his clothing, a neatness that was getting to be more irrelevant by the passing moment in the present circumstances.

At the rear of the burnt-out building a low-sided wagon was parked. It had the name of the Winton newspaper painted on the sides and a board above the seat backrest. It was almost unscathed by the fire: sprinkled with ash and soot and a little scarred by some burning debris that had fallen on to it. Edge did not bother dusting off the seat before he climbed aboard the rig and sat down. Faced across the blackened rubble, rested the rifle on his thighs. He struck a match on the stock of the Winchester, again relit the neglected cigarette. Wondered inconsequentially if he should quit smoking. Then, as he became more keenly aware of the coldness of the air, how the taint of last night's explosion and fire still permeated it, he experienced an almost painful desire for a cup of strong, hot coffee.

'What now?' McCloud asked as he leaned against a front wheel of the wagon and surveyed the scene of destruction with baleful eyes.

'We wait for them, Doc.'

'You realise, of course, we won't surprise them? They'll see your horse over there on the street and suspect somebody is waiting here, surely?'

Edge replied evenly: 'If I planned to surprise anyone by being here, I wouldn't have rode down the middle of the street, large as life and twice as ugly, Doc.'

The old man uttered a small sound of disgust then muttered: 'You don't intend to tell me your plans?'

'Don't have any until I see what I'm up against.'

'*We're* up against, remember?' McCloud snapped.

'Sure, Doc. But it's still the same situation. Until they make their move, there's no point trying to guess what it'll be.'

McCloud thought about it as he shifted his morose gaze back and forth over the rubble, found he kept being drawn to look at the one black and two white nooses hanging from the gantry: closer to where he and Edge waited than to the street where the condemned couple would be brought from the meeting hall.

Then he vented a despairing sound. And shivered, like for the first time he felt cold in the neat suit that was hardly adequate protection for his emaciated frame on such a brightly sunlit but bitingly frosty morning.

He turned his back on the fire rubble, to peer out over the rolling hill country of the Beaver Valley's eastern flank. Where the scattered farmsteads at this time of the year were surrounded by ploughed fields waiting for the spring planting of crops. Each farmhouse had a smoking chimney and here and there men and women were out on their properties, attending to the winter chores. Perhaps ignorant of, or maybe simply uncaring about, the troubles of the town.

'Winton was such a fine, proud place to live in until we discovered what an awful mistake we made at the trial of John Grady,' the frail-looking doctor said at length, without turning toward the half-breed.

Edge said: 'Judge Benedict told me as much, Doc.'

McCloud went on in the same detached tone: 'I'm not claiming we haven't had our troubles before. Some of them of a serious nature. But not so many to merit us having a courthouse and regular calls from circuit judges. That was only because we had hopes of becoming the county seat at one time.'

He sighed, asked: 'You know something, Mr Edge?'

'About what?'

'Winton. The way it is now, this morning, despicable as this situation is, at least it's being taken care of in Winton's way—as it were?'

A degree of pride had entered his tone as he kept his back to the town of which he was talking, concentrated his gaze on the open countryside. 'It is being done with decorum, wouldn't you agree?'

Edge growled: 'Yeah, if a lynch mob can have decorum, I guess this one has it.'

McCloud shot a glance at Edge hunched up on the wagon seat, scowled at the cynical tone of his response. Then quickly turned his head again like he was concerned he might catch a peripheral glimpse of the line of three nooses.

'There was no rabble rousing, was there?' he retorted

defensively. 'You even slept through it all.'

'We've already struck a bargain, Doc,' Edge muttered. 'You don't have to sell me on anything else.'

McCloud chose to ignore the wryly voiced reply. Explained: 'When people found out Nicholas had released Grady for a second time, after he'd admitted he shot one of the O'Hara brothers, and Mrs Graham even though she had said she was in the newspaper building shortly before it was destroyed, people were naturally worried. That's when some of them took the first steps toward a lynching. Behind closed doors. Without fuss. No raucous protests.'

Despite his impatience with the ramblings of the old man who felt such a compulsive need to justify the actions of his fellow citizens, Edge involuntarily thought back to the early hours of the morning. When he left the law office and headed back to the hotel, his mind concerned with what Alvin Ridler had said: coming to terms with the idea he would have to start caring what people thought of him if he were to find a place where it was possible to put down roots.

While his mind was thus engaged, his guard had obviously been down. For he had failed to be aware the town around him was not locked up as tight as it looked: everyone cowering silently in their private worlds of terror. Somewhere along the silent streets, behind firmly shut doors and drawn drapes, men and women had been tensely waiting and watching. To see if anyone else except Edge and the sheriff left the law office: to be turned loose into a community where four men held responsible for the wrongful hanging of John Grady had already died violently.

'Figure they went about it like they were treading on eggs, Doc,' Edge growled. And was suddenly struck by a notion that could explain why he slept so long and soundly this strange morning: not about to be awakened prematurely by anything short of an earthquake. Maybe this was because for the first time he could remember, he had slept the sleep of a perfectly contented man?

McCloud was saying: '... I watched them bring Fletcher Grady and Mrs Graham down the street. Even as they were taken to the meeting hall, surely knew something of what was happening, they made no protest.'

'Maybe they were struck dumb with terror, Doc.'

'That could have been so,' McCloud allowed absently, then sighed and turned away from looking out over the rolling hills featured with the scattered farms, squinted up at Edge to ask: 'Mind telling me something, sir?'

Edge shrugged.

'When you failed to emerge from the hotel for so long, I thought you were like the other guests there: had been persuaded to remain apart from the troubles of this town which you are only passing through. Even when you came out of the livery with your horse, I had my doubts I would be able to convince you to help us. But you did. I'd be interested to know just why you agreed so readily to do so?'

Edge patted his sheepskin coat as he said: 'A hundred dollars, Doc.'

McCloud shook his head irritably at the facile response. But managed to check an impulse to scowl before he said: 'No matter how flush a man is, the prospect of more money to bolster his stake is always welcome. But I don't think that's the sole reason in this case, sir.'

'If it isn't, it's the only reason that's any business of yours, Doc,' Edge told him. In part because he had no wish to go into the convoluted reasoning that turned performing some kind of civic service in Winton into practice for being a good citizen some place else. But mostly it was because he did not want to be distracted from the sounds he could now hear: out on the street, down toward the intersection of Travis with Juniper.

McCloud asked tensely: 'Is it starting?'

Edge glanced down at the crinkled face, upturned to show an anxiously quizzical expression as the old man recognised something had changed in Edge's attitude.

'My hearing's not what it once was, sir.'

'They're coming this way, Doc,' Edge said, shifted his gaze to the front corner of the drugstore where the group of people he could hear would first come into view. Then he pumped the lever action of the Winchester to jack a shell into the breech, cock the hammer.

McCloud straightened up against the wheel, looked fixedly at the same spot as Edge and swallowed dryly, then craned forward, straining his dulled hearing to catch the first sound of the approaching people before his unblinking eyes saw them.

They came at a slow, measured pace and it would have been easy for a vivid imagination to think in terms of a party of mourners going through the motions of a funeral: while the subjects to be interred were still alive, able to play their parts in the macabre rehearsal.

There was no talk. Just the out of step shuffling of feet on hard-packed dirt.

A sharp intake of breath signalled when McCloud heard this.

'There's something I neglected to tell you, sir.'

Edge shifted one hand off the rifle, took the cigarette from the side of his mouth. From habit nipped out the glowing flakes of tobacco between a thumb and forefinger before he arced the butt away, into the charred rubble.

'I give the rumour no credence,' the old man went on, 'but some think Nicholas used Vernon Bassett and Miss Cannon's departure as an excuse. That he left Winton because he's afraid.'

'No sweat, Doc,' Edge said, dropped his hand back to fist it around the barrel of the rifle as the first member of the group on the street came into sight.

It was Ernie O'Mally, the powerfully-built blacksmith. He was tugging on the end of a length of rope. Just behind him was the tall and lean Bill Henderson who also gripped some rope which stretched out behind him at waist height with a slight curve of slack.

Henderson's skinny wife was beside him. Then Edge recognised Jeremiah Harman, the saloon-keeper. For the next few moments concentrated his impassive attention on just two figures while the rest did not chance a glance to the side: like they were afraid to glimpse the nooses.

The pair he watched were unable to look in any direction, because both had black fabric sacks over their heads, loosely fastened at their throats.

Even if he had not known the circumstances which triggered the lynch mob into existence, Edge would have recognised the hooded pair who were led by the wrists bound in front of them: from the shabby duster worn by Fletcher Grady, the black cape of Roxanne Graham.

Then he recognised three of the old-timers who had been in the Oregon Trail Saloon last night. Shannon and Drew, two of the drummers staying at the Winton Hotel, but not the razor-slashed Roy Elrick. Some of the others in the group of twenty or so men and a few women he had seen watching the fire or helping to put it out.

All of them were warmly wrapped up for the frosty morning, mutely exhaling misted breath as they came to a ragged halt, gathered closely around the condemned couple and turned to stare across the fire detritus at the gantry with the three nooses suspended from it.

Some of them gasped and all of them changed expression when they saw Edge sitting on the wagon, McCloud standing beside it.

Now the dragging of feet on the street was ended, a woman could be heard softly weeping. Plainly this was the helpless Roxanne Graham, the sounds of her despair muffled by the sack over her head.

If the just as helpless Fletcher Grady tried to give her any words of comfort, they were not spoken loudly enough through the hood to carry across the acridly malodorous rubble to the wagon. Nobody else spoke for stretched seconds. Then, after apprehensive glances were traded within the group, Bill Henderson complained croakily:

'You shouldn't be here, Mr Mayor. You said you weren't going to have a hand in this.'

McCloud confirmed in funereal tones: 'That is correct, sir. I said I would have no part in a lynching. You all can see I am not here in the capacity of mayor to prevent such a lynching.'

'Can see your badge, Doctor McCloud,' O'Mally countered. He seemed to try for scorn, but was unable to totally conceal something of the deference with which he treated the old man in normal circumstances.

'What's the idea of swearin' in that hard-nosed stranger as a deputy?' Jeremiah Harman snarled. Probably he would not treat the President of the United States with any degree of respect unless he was a high-spending customer of the Oregon Trail.

Roxanne Graham was no longer weeping under the hood. Stood rigid and silent, straining to hear every word of the exchange. Like Grady beside her. The two of them surely wondering if they dared to hope they were to survive.

'He don't scare me, badge or no badge!'

This was snarled by a man who had emerged from the rear corner of the McIver Drugstore. Despite his voice being muffled, much as the weeping of the condemned woman had been, Edge knew who made the boast that was followed by the order:

'Toss the Winchester away, Edge! And don't you do anything foolish, Doc.'

Now Edge turned just his head to look at Roy Elrick as the drummer advanced a few paces along the side of the drugstore: aimed a Frontier Colt at arm's length. It was an identical revolver to the one in Edge's holster. But much newer, even brand new from the way its oiled surfaces gleamed in the frosty sunlight.

The reason for Elrick's muffled tone was that his lower face was swathed in bandages that encircled his head, just his brow and eyes below the brim of his derby and his nostrils and mouth uncovered. But the dressing was bound tightly enough to restrict the movement of his lips and this impaired his speech.

He thumbed back the hammer of the Colt without causing the barrel of the big sixshooter to waver from its aim at Edge's head. And the half-breed knew Roy Elrick was no stranger to handguns as he said evenly:

'He doesn't like to be called Doc. And I don't like to have guns aimed at me, feller. Give that warning when I can.'

'You think I give a damn about that, mister?' There was harsh menace in the muffled voice. 'I told you, toss the rifle away!'

'Why would I do that?' Edge asked.

It started a buzz of talk among the lynch mob delayed from

141

carrying out its purpose. From witnessing their initial mute reaction, the half-breed was certain Elrick showing up was as much a surprise to them as to him and McCloud.

'Guns are my business, mister!' the drummer snapped. 'And that's a warning, you better believe. I sell them for a living. I know about them. I can shoot them well. I'm not fast, like your kind, Edge. But I'm accurate. And since I have this weapon in my hand and aimed at the target, I don't have to be fast.'

'You left out something, feller,' Edge told him evenly.

'Uh?' The comment and the way it was delivered mildly perturbed Elrick. But the Colt did not move a fraction of an inch in the rock-steady grip at the end of his outstretched arm.

Edge unfolded slowly to his feet, the Winchester held loosely in both hands: so that when he causally half turned, the muzzle swung. Its aim raked along the side wall of the drugstore until it came to bear on the man who sold guns for a living and knew much about them.

'Toss it away, I told you!' the bandaged man snarled through the restricted opening in the dressing.

Either Shannon or Drew yelled: 'Don't trust that sonofabitch, Roy!'

Edge squeezed the trigger of the Winchester an instant after his hands fisted more tightly around the barrel and frame. The report was shockingly loud in the strangely quiet morning, echoed among the buildings of the terrified town.

A hole appeared in the centre of Elrick's forehead and he was jerked backwards by the impact of the high velocity rifle shot at such short range. His collapsing corpse banged into the drugstore wall, bounced off it. Blood oozed from the hole in the front of his head, splashed down to stain the white bandage below. Much more blood, brain matter and bone splinters sprayed out through the exit wound to leave a larger stain on the wall as he fell forward, hit the ground face down and lay utterly still.

The rifle shot had curtailed the subdued sounds from the Old Town area of Winton behind the row of stores. The roan gelding whinnied, tried to wrench free of the hitching rail but gave up and resumed the same kind of uneasy silence as before.

McCloud scuttled around the rear of the wagon, muttering incomprehensibly, and stooped down beside the obviously dead man.

'He didn't say he could shoot to kill,' Edge announced flatly as he turned, pumped the action of the rifle, aimed it in the general direction of the awesomely silent group, frozen by shock on the other side of the rubble. 'I do that sometimes.'

One of the old-timer saloon customers accused bitterly: 'You deputised a cold-blooded killer like him, McCloud?'

'I can be that sometimes,' Edge said in the same tone as before. 'When somebody's trying to kill me. If somebody's aiming a gun at me, I have to figure that's what he has in mind.'

'Killing wasn't a part of our arrangement!' the town doctor complained as he rose from beside Elrick, gazed despairingly across at the huddle of people on Travis Street, then malevolently at Edge. He shivered, perhaps from the cold.

'How many more of us to do you plan to kill, Edge?' Bill Henderson challenged with grim determination.

His defiant attitude was not matched by the rest of the group. Most of them directed anxious glances at him, then gazed fearfully at the half-breed again, when Edge responded:

'As many as it takes: from when the Doc tells you to turn the prisoners loose.'

McCloud made a spluttering sound as he struggled to find his voice.

Henderson looked desperately around, found himself alone in his challenge to Edge. Nobody would look at him and some of those on the fringe of the group that was no longer a lynch mob even shuffled sheepishly away. But the hotel owner drew some comfort from his wife when she fastened a grip on his upper arm.

'I'm going to call your bluff, mister!' he insisted. 'These murders have to stop before half the population of Winton is dead! And we can only be sure they will if those responsible are executed!'

He took a step forward, drawing taut the slack in the length of rope tied to the wrists of Roxanne Graham.

A choked cry sounded under the hood.

Kath Henderson gasped, tightened her grip on her husband's arm.

Fletcher Grady pleaded from within his hood: 'Roxanne and me didn't do no killin's!'

Edge threw the stock of the Winchester against his shoulder, aligned the sights on Bill Henderson's narrow chest, said loudly enough for everyone to hear above the buzz of shocked exclamations as people backed away from the threatened man: 'You're the top hand, Doc.'

'No!' McCloud shrieked. 'I cannot condone such a thing!'

'That's a good decision, Mr Mayor,' a woman said from the rear of the drugstore where Elrick had appeared.

'Mary!' Henderson called in a strangled tone.

'You must let them go, father,' she told him.

'Girl, we've talked it through and we're sure they——'

'Delmar Crocker's dead,' she cut in on him.

'Miss Mary say Delmar Crocker?' one of the old-timers asked of O'Mally. 'Shit, he was on the jury!'

'Dead the same way as the others?' a woman demanded tremulously.

'Drowned in one of the troughs in his corral, Mrs Brannigan,' came the monotone response. 'Right, Lieutenant Nolan?'

Edge eased the rifle down from his shoulder until it was angled across the front of his body. Turned just his head to see where Mary Henderson stood beside the infantry officer who with his wife and children was a guest at the Winton Hotel. She was wearing an all-enveloping topcoat and he had on his full uniform. When he had nodded in agreement with what she claimed, she gestured toward the line of nooses suspended from the gantry, added:

'One of those things fixed in the open doorway of a stable.'

'That could have been done last night before——' her father started.

'No, sir,' Nolan cut in. 'The water's pretty icy in the trough, so the body's not warm. But it's not cold enough for the man to have been dead much more than a few minutes before we found him, I'd say.'

His uniform was still damp from where he had tested the temperature of the corpse in the trough: maybe lifted it out of the water.

'Oh, my God!' McCloud gasped. 'You people almost...'

The looks on the faces of many members of the group no longer gathered so closely around the hooded and bound pair showed they either spoke something similar to what the doctor could not bring himself to conclude: or were stunned into silent shock by the very thought of it.

'Damn it, Bill!' O'Mally blurted at length. 'All them stables face across the street from the back of Delmar's corral. If there'd been a hanging rope in a doorway, we'd have been sure to see it when we came outta the meetin' hall!'

'Yeah!' Mrs Brannigan agreed. 'Far as I recall, all the doors were closed up then.'

There was a muttering of agreement with this. Which ended abruptly when O'Mally turned, dropped the rope he had been holding, started to unfasten the other end from the wrists of Fletcher Grady.

Then a woman started to release the wrists of Roxanne Graham as Kath Henderson gently removed the other end of the rope from the grasp of her husband. Henderson seemed totally numbed by shock, not comprehending anything of what was happening to him and around him.

Edge eased the hammer of the Winchester forward, canted the barrel to his shoulder as McCloud said morosely:

'If only you got here a few moments earlier, Miss Henderson.'

'We came as quickly as we could after finding the drowned man,' the infantry lieutenant replied defensively. 'I'll allow we kept our approach surreptitious. Since we didn't want to alarm people into doing something prematurely. But we didn't realise any other lives were at risk.'

Mary Henderson seemed not to have heard the remark addressed to her, nor the army man's hurried response. Her gaze remained fixed on the inert form of the face down Roy Elrick, a grimace giving her mouth an ugly line.

There was a babble of low-toned talk from the group on the street as the hoods were removed from the heads of Grady and Roxanne. Then the former lynch mob reduced to a shamefaced group of misguided ordinary people began to disperse. Slowly at first, then more quickly. Just a few held back to offer inadequate apologies to the reprieved couple. Who could not, or just did not trust themselves to speak as they stood close together, unsteadily, an arm around each other.

'If only I hadn't given a badge to such a man,' McCloud said, perhaps involuntarily voicing his thoughts. His sparsely fleshed, deeply lined face expressed a harsher brand of contempt than he was able to generate in his voice as he watched Edge climb down off the wagon: maybe shared the powerful emotion between the half-breed and himself.

Lieutenant Nolan shifted his empty-eyed gaze from the body of Elrick to Edge as the half-breed removed the badge from his coat, said: 'It's pretty far ranging. If only the Almighty hadn't created the world there wouldn't be any evil. Or good.'

Edge moved away from the wagon and held out the badge toward McCloud. Who snatched it back and looked sick to his stomach as he insisted:

'There was no need for it! You dishonoured this peace officer's badge, sir!'

He hurled the tin star forcefully into the nearest pile of blackened rubble so the impact spurted up dust and soot.

'You couldn't know it was going to turn out to be a personal matter between Roy and Edge, Doctor McCloud,' Mary Henderson said sympathetically, then glanced acrimoniously at the half-breed.

Edge had to make a considerable conscious effort to sustain an impassive façade while a turmoil of conflicting emotions came and went through his mind. Predominant of these was a dangerously overheated anger at Mary Henderson for the implication he had put a hole in Elrick's head in some kind of duel over her. He said, just a little tautly: 'The feller should have let things lay.'

'He wouldn't have shot you!'

This was snarled by either Shannon or Drew as the two city-suited, derby-hatted drummers advanced along the former alley.

Now just Fletcher Grady and Roxanne Graham were left out on the street, still embracing each other.

'He was no killer,' Shannon growled.

'He just sold guns,' Drew augmented morosely.

'Like he said, he made a living at it,' Edge allowed, dug for the makings.

'Right,' Drew agreed, the scowl of scorn becoming more firmly fixed on his cherubic face. 'He made his living selling them, was all.'

Edge drawled as he turned away from the group around the corpse: 'And they say a man who lives by the gun will die by the gun.'

14

By the time Edge had taken the long way around the blackened rubble from the rear of the former newspaper building, smoke was wisping from the chimney of the cafe outside which he had hitched his gelding.

While he made his sluggish way toward the cafe, called René's Place, beyond the line of stores, rolling then lighting a cigarette, moves were being made to eradicate all traces of the new violence which had exploded in Winton.

At first there was a brief disagreement between the abruptly officious McCloud and the two smoulderingly angry drummers. During which the names of Frank Behan and Delmar Crocker were often mentioned before the elderly man, who looked close to exhaustion by then, gave in. Allowed Shannon and Drew to pick up the body and take it away, the dead man's own suit jacket draped over his blood-stained head as he was carried along Travis Street.

Following a briefer, far less heated exchange, Lieutenant Nolan agreed to help Mary Henderson and went with her, picking his way more carefully than she through the fire detritus toward the gantry. There the army man took out a clasp knife, stood twice on the crate brought there for the lynchings and cut through the ropes.

By then, McCloud had gotten to where Grady and Roxanne continued to stand in frozen attitudes, still embracing and not talking: like they were too shocked to begin to function again outside of involuntarily taking in and letting out their breath.

Edge ignored what was happening around him until, after he had slid the Winchester back in the boot, he checked his move to unhitch the gelding's reins when a woman spoke to him.

'*Bonjour, monsieur.* It is my opinion you did what was right. *Trés bon!*'

The thickly accented greeting and opinion were offered by an enormously fat woman in the doorway of the cafe who gazed approvingly at the half-breed. He thought she probably weighed close to two hundred and fifty pounds, packed on to a five and a half feet tall frame. She was past forty or maybe more than fifty: had a youthful looking face but above this the thin grey hair aged her. Excess flesh hung on her facial bone structure in a way that created curves which gave her a cheerful countenance.

Edge found her smile engaging after the events of the strangely quiet morning had come to such an explosive culmination.

'I won't argue with you about that, ma'am,' he said and stroked the neck of his horse, the animal much calmer since Winton had resumed the quiet activities of everyday small town life. 'Tell you something else?'

'*Monsieur?*'

'That coffee is starting to smell like the best thing could happen to me today.'

She emphasised the curves of her natural smile lines, told him eagerly: '*Dix minutes, monsieur.*' Held up both pudgy hands, fat fingers splayed. 'Ten, *oui*? A little more time you wait, I can make you *le petit déjeuner.* Breakfast, *oui*? Anerican style?'

'Coffee is all.'

'*Café, oui.*' She nodded vigorously, altered her expression to concern. 'The appetite for eating, it is not so good after . . .' She moved a big hand to encompass the scene across the street. 'You will come inside Renés Place, *monsieur. Dix minutes, café français* style. *Trés* strong.'

The fat woman, grinning again, backed into the cafe that was getting to smell more appealing by the moment. And Fletcher Grady asked:

'You mind if I make that my treat, Mr Edge?'

The half-breed turned toward the man who had been close to summary execution a few minutes ago. Grady sounded exhausted, but managed to spread a weak smile across his

149

ashen face as he advanced on Edge. Roxanne was clasping his arm almost desperately, like she was afraid she might not be able to keep from keeling over without this support.

'No, feller,' Edge told him impassively, saw the fragile smile instantly vanish before he added: 'You don't owe me anything. I was well paid for doing what I did.'

He looked beyond the couple, saw the immediate vicinity of the newspaper building where just the blackened cable noose remained as a macabre reminder of the ramifications of the fire's morning aftermath was deserted, except for the three of them out front of the cafe. For the rest of its length, up to the church and cemetery at the distant southern end, everything appeared normal for this time of morning in a prosperous country town.

Ralph McCloud, Lieutenant Nolan and Mary Henderson were among the people starting to go about their daily business. But Shannon and Drew were no longer in sight, apparently had taken a short cut on one of the side streets to get their burden to Frank Behan's funeral parlour on Juniper.

'We'd like to pay you what we can afford to do another job, mister,' Roxanne Graham said tentatively.

She did not look her best. Her blonde hair was disarrayed from being under the hood and there had been no time for her to apply the usual morning paints and powders to her puffy face before she was forcibly taken from her home to the meeting hall. To endure the anguish of the vigilante court, the harrowing events that followed, then the draining relief of being saved from the noose at the last moment.

All this had left her looking many years older than Edge recalled from when he last saw her in the law office.

'Plan to leave town just as soon as I've had a cup of that good-smelling coffee,' he said, turned to step into the small cafe that was far neater and cleaner on the inside than was promised by its shabby façade.

It was a small room, overcrowded with just a half dozen tables each with four chairs at it. The tables were draped with red and white checkered covers. An open doorway in a rear corner emanated steam which carried the aroma of brewing coffee.

Roxanne Graham looked dejected.

'Won't do no harm to hear us out, Mr Edge?' Grady urged, half resentful, half pleading, as he trailed the half-breed into the tiny cafe.

Roxanne had to release his arm at the doorway, but she stayed very close to him: like a frightened child anxious not to get too far away from a parent in a crowd. Then, with the door firmly closed on the town returning to normal, she gained in confidence, called out brightly:

'Morning, Marie! Make that three cups of coffee, will you?'

'It will be my pleasure, after you have the *formidable* experience, *madame*!' the fat woman called, sincere concern and eagerness to please in her tone.

Edge had already sat at a table in the rear corner of the room across from the kitchen doorway. Chose the chair that gave him a view of the solid door to the street and the curtained window beside it. He took off his hat, put it on the table, nodded his assent to the couple and motioned to the other chairs at the table.

'I'd like . . . That is, Roxanne and me want you to find out who's killin' all these people, Edge,' Grady said, sat down without waiting for Roxanne to take a chair. 'A man don't make enough money to have enough to spare to salt away when he only does odd jobs for folks. But Roxanne, she can raise some cash to pay you for your trouble.'

In the kitchen, Marie had started to sing softly. Her voice seemed surprisingly sweet and melodious for a woman with such a massive build. But there was a lack of spontaneity in the tuneful song she sang in her native language: like she was pointedly trying to bring cheer to her place to which three people had cause to create an atmosphere of gloom and despondency, at the same time tried to keep herself from listening to what was being said.

'I turned in my deputy's badge,' Edge reminded them, managed to revive life in the cigarette before it died at the side of his mouth.

'The law's been no damn use to us this far, mister, like you well know!' Grady muttered morosely.

Roxanne said with greater force, the scowl on her fleshy

face raising colour to her cheeks: 'With that sonofabitch Kenyon running scared, and McCloud too long in the tooth to be any good as a deputy, the law sure as hell ain't going to be any use now!'

'It's just a rumour the sheriff won't be comin' back,' Grady told her tautly.

'Which I happen to believe, Fletch!' she snapped adamantly, like she was ready to launch into a bitter argument over the point if Grady wanted to press the challenge.

Edge was impassively content during the silence while the woman in the once elegant cloak waited for a reaction from the man whose duster had not been designed for smartness.

Rather than fuel the fires of a disagreement that had no place in such a situation, Grady directed an expression of concern for Roxanne, seemed worried her impulse to anger was a bad sign of how she intended to overcome the traumatic effects of the morning's events. Then there was resignation on his pale and haggard face as he allowed: 'You could be right.'

He was briefly relieved when she acknowledged this with a curt nod, sat back with her arms folded, prepared to let him do the talking. For as long, anyway, as he said what she wanted to hear. Then he said to Edge:

'I reckon Delmar Crocker getting killed when he did means me and Roxanne are safe now, Mr Edge? After what almost happened to us . . .'

He absently raised a hand and gingerly massaged his throat with a thumb and forefinger, his Adam's apple bobbing. 'I don't guess anyone will even give us so much as a dirty look for a long while to come. And we sure can't be on the list of people this crazy killer is sendin' to the promised land for what they done to get Curly hung. Seein' as how me and Roxanne were about the only ones around here didn't figure my boy was guilty.'

'Time's wasting, Fletch,' Roxanne urged as sounds of the coffee being poured emerged from the kitchen and Marie's singing faded, faltered and ended. She leaned toward Edge to emphasise the depth of her feelings. 'See, Fletch doesn't want anyone else to die on account of what happened to his son.

Nor neither do I. Not least because I want to see Fletch able to hold his head up as high as anyone else in this town.'

'I thought you said time was waste——' Grady tried to cut in.

Roxanne waved a dismissive hand at him, pressed on: 'Which he won't be able to do, long as people are being murdered because Curly was hung. But if he's known to be behind the man who finds the one who's been doing all the killing, then that'll wipe the slate well and truly clean, I'd say?'

She looked at Grady, her eyes starting to gleam with excitement at the thought.

He shrugged and nodded without enthusiasm as the big French-speaking woman came into the room carrying a tray bearing three fragrantly steaming cups, agreed: 'That's about the size of it, I guess.'

Roxanne leaned close to Edge and lowered her voice to a rasping whisper so it would not carry to Marie, said: 'And the exact size of the fee I can go to to pay for Fletch's peace of mind is one thousand dollars, Mr Edge.' Then she sat back in her chair, told him dolefully: 'The bakery business doesn't make a person rich, but it lets me put a little away for a rainy day every now and then. I can get that much out of Caldwell's bank just as soon as you give the word.' She grimaced as she concluded: 'The new ovens I was planning will have to wait.'

Then, in case this remark made Grady feel bad, she reached across and squeezed his hand. Had to break the contact when the fat woman delivered the three cups of coffee to the table.

Marie grinned, bobbed her head and murmured something politely dismissive in French after Edge nodded and the other two patrons of her small cafe spoke brief words of gratitude.

Because the good-smelling coffee was yet too hot to drink, Edge ignored his better judgement and submitted to an impulse to respond to the eagerly inquisitive gazes of Roxanne and Grady.

'You got any idea who'd feel so strongly about the way the boy was hanged for a killing he didn't do?'

Grady suddenly looked deeply dejected, shook his head and glanced helplessly at Roxanne. She said:

'Don't think we haven't given it plenty of thought, Mr

Edge. I know I was thinking harder about it than anything else in my whole life before. While those crazy people were getting ready to bring us out of the meeting hall to string us up.'

'And Kenyon was a pretty good lawman until he got scared and took off last night,' Grady said. 'So I reckon he did some wrackin' of his brains.'

Roxanne nodded, reached across to touch his hand again while she murmured: 'But it has to be said: because this is no time for pussyfooting around, right Fletch?'

'Say whatever you like, if it'll help any,' he assured.

'Curly Grady wasn't the best liked of young men around Winton, Mr Edge.'

The boy's father said dejectedly: 'I ain't gonna deny it, because it'd be a lie if I did. Curly was a loner all his life, right from the time he was little. He never made no friends on account of he never went out of his way to get anyone to like him.'

As Grady shrugged his narrow shoulders, Edge consciously kept his mind from filling with notions that he and the unjustly executed youngster had something in common. He had made more than enough self-discoveries since he rode into this town.

Grady was saying: 'I dunno, maybe John was the kinda son only a parent could like. And there were times, when he was at his worst, even I couldn't stand the sight of him. His Ma, too, when she was alive.' He sighed, added: 'I'm ashamed to admit.'

Marie made to go into the kitchen, then halted with a gasp. Which drew all attention to that corner of the cafe as Mary Henderson emerged from the doorway.

She said breathlessly, like she'd been running to get to the rear of the building: 'That was the reason so many thought he was guilty of strangling the girl almost from the moment her body was found.'

Edge, tense behind impassiveness, had shifted his glinting-eyed gaze quickly to the unclear view of the street through the curtained window beside the door.

Mary saw this, realised he was suspicious of her sudden

appearance in the cafe after entering it from the rear. She told him: 'I'm alone. But you're right to be worried, Edge. There are likely to be quite a few others coming here pretty soon. If some hotheads have their way. And I'm afraid my father will be the ringleader again.'

'Shit!' Grady groaned, shook his head, hurried to say: 'Excuse me, ladies. What now, Miss Mary?'

Roxanne looked like she was about to lose control of her new found confidence as she blurted: 'Surely nobody can still think we had anything to do with——'

'I'm afraid they can, Roxanne,' Mary broke in, her expression getting graver by the moment as she recovered from over-exertion. 'After Barny Drew and Glen Shannon get through planting the notion in their heads.'

'But they all had to admit we couldn't have had anything to do with Delmar Crocker's killing!' the older woman exclaimed hoarsely. 'They know they had me and Fletcher over in the meeting hall when it happened!'

'Tryin' everythin' short of beatin' up on us to make us confess!' Grady snarled, the prospect of more trouble finally triggering a vehement response to the morning's terrifying events from him. 'And when they couldn't, the bastards dragged us through the streets to hang us anyway! Without nobody else in this lousy town doin' anythin' to stop them until Edge——'

His high emotions—a mixture of rage, remembered terror and fear for the immediate future as he kept glancing at the door to the street—combined to trap the protest in his pulsing throat.

Mary Henderson nodded several times while he was blurting out the increasingly shrill words. Explained immediately his voice failed him: 'They all know that, Mr Grady. Maybe they wouldn't have believed me. But as luck would have it, when I went to the meeting hall to try to talk my father and the rest out of their madness, Lieutenant Nolan was going to the corral. To get his team and wagon so he could leave town with his wife and children. They had to accept his word Mr Crocker only just drowned before we found him in the trough. That made it clear you two couldn't have killed him and fixed up the noose in the doorway the way it was.'

'So I'm elected the next candidate for stringing up?' Edge drawled. Was the first to try the cooling coffee and found it bitter instead of strong to his taste.

'What?' Roxanne gasped.

'Uh?' Grady grunted, looking even more perplexed than she did.

'That's right,' Mary answered. 'You've experienced how the people of this town grasp at the easiest explanation for whatever they can't fully understand. The way they sentenced John Grady to be hanged. Would have lynched Mrs Graham and Mr Grady if you and Ralph McCloud hadn't intervened. You look like their idea of a hired killer, Edge. And you were seen to shoot down Roy Elrick without turning a hair.'

'Mon Dieu!' Marie exclaimed. She looked balefully, then fearfully at Edge, shook her head and forced Mary Henderson to step out of her path as she hustled into the kitchen, began to mutter in her own language.

'But that's stupid!' Roxanne snapped.

'It's friggin' crazy is what it is!' Grady snarled, straightened up from the table and knocked his chair over backwards. 'We ain't the kind to send for no gunslinger! We wouldn't know how, damnit!'

'It turned out your son wasn't the kind to kill Teresa Ward,' Mary reminded as Roxanne rose less forcefully from her chair. This time she took a grip on Grady's arm to placate his reckless rage rather than to draw comfort for her own shattered nerves.

Edge dropped his cigarette butt into the hardly touched coffee. Its few remaining glowing embers made little sound as they were doused and he said flatly: 'I can see how it looks if people want to look at it that way.'

'People terrified of getting slaughtered will clutch at any straw,' Mary said.

'But——' Roxanne tried to interject.

'I got to town just before the killing started,' Edge cut her off. 'They could figure that was no coincidence.'

Mary said: 'My mother was in the hotel dining room with

156

you when Judge Benedict was shot. But if she tries to vouch for you and they even bother to listen to her, they could convince each other Mr Grady or Mrs Graham got things started with the judge.'

'But none of us could've done that to Crocker!' Grady insisted vehemently. 'They know where Roxanne and me were. And Edge was with McCloud, damnit! Surely they ain't gonna figure McCloud'd have anythin' to do with——'

'I don't know!' Mary broke in, disinterested in rationalisations concerned with what she had come here to reveal. 'I just heard those two salesmen friends of Roy talking to my father and Mr O'Mally and some others who had a hand in what happened at the meeting hall and across the street this morning.'

Edge said: 'And after the way that all ended, they're ready to believe anything that'll make them feel better. Especially if it shows they weren't so far wrong in what they thought.'

'You could have strangled Mr McCormack at the hotel, Edge' Mary pointed out. 'After you fixed it for the newspaper building to blow up with one of the O'Hara brothers inside.'

'I could have,' he allowed.

'And you admitted to the sheriff and Mr Ridler saw it, that you fired the first bullet into the other O'Hara brother. Before Mr Grady made sure he was dead. That's what Shannon and Drew are saying. And they won't need many willing listeners to swallow that before there's another lynch mob formed. And it won't matter they can't prove you did the other killings. Jack O'Hara will be enough. Along with how you shot Roy Elrick in front of so many of them. Shot him with such, such...'

She eyed Edge with a manufactured scowl, in back of which was a kind of regret, as she completed: 'Such a total lack of compassion.'

'About the same way he would have shot me, I had to figure,' Edge said.

She barked back at him: 'I told you I knew Roy well! And I agree with what his friends said. He was no killer! He wouldn't have shot you!'

Edge countered evenly: 'Anyone who isn't ready to shoot a

man shouldn't aim a gun at him, lady.'

'What does any of this matter?' Roxanne growled anxiously. She let go of Grady's arm, moved quickly between the tables to reach the window. 'If that same bunch of crazy people are fixing to finish what you kept them from doing, we oughta be thinking of what to do about it, seems to me, mister!'

She jerked aside the curtain to look out of the window. But even when she pressed the side of her head to the glass, the angle was too narrow. She muttered something in the tone of a curse, swung to the door.

'It matters to me,' Edge said to the room in general. 'I don't kill for the hell of it. Just like I don't hire on to kill. If that ain't registered in people's minds, I can see how they might think what they do about why I came to Winton.'

'We weren't gonna give you a grand to——' Grady started to protest.

Edge rose to his feet, delved into a pants pocket, jingled some coins.

'He knows that!' Roxanne snapped as she jerked open the door.

Grady blurted: 'We just wanted you to do what Kenyon couldn't, mister! Find out who's been killin' all these people around here!'

'It still looks pretty normal out there,' Roxanne reported, calming now, from where she stood on the threshold of the open doorway, cold air streaming in as she leaned out, peered southward along Travis Street.

'Maybe they won't come here,' Mary allowed with a shrug. 'Maybe they won't do anything after all. There could be enough level headed people left in this town to talk sense into the others. Stop them repeating the same stupidity as this morning.'

She had started out talking like she was trying to convince herself that what she was saying was a possibility. Until a note of hysteria crept into her voice as she went on quickly: 'Maybe I was stupid, to sneak down here and warn you, but I thought——'

'I'm obliged you took the trouble,' Edge told her, peered at the bill of fare chalked on a blackboard on the wall beside the door at the kitchen. He left a nickel on the table to cover the cost of just one coffee, raised his voice to call toward the corner doorway: 'And I'm obliged to you, ma'am.'

The fat woman waddled out of the kitchen with the same tray as before. Clearly she had been listening to the talk in her cafe, and had not liked what she overheard. Her face wore a deep frown that negated the cheerful curves of the excess flesh. But although it was plain she was scowlingly anxious to have these people leave her establishment before they brought their trouble here, pride in her culinary skills did not allow her to overlook that two cups of coffee had not been touched, a third contained the disintegrating remains of a cigarette butt.

She made a throaty sound of disgust, then complained as she rattled the cups on the tray, spilled some coffee in the process: 'You have no need to thank me for what you do not enjoy, *monsieur*.'

'I'm obliged you took the trouble,' Edge answered evenly. 'I can't be sure there's anything wrong with your French style coffee, ma'am. It could just be I've lost my taste for everything about this town.'

He put on his hat, tipped it in farewell to the disgruntled fat woman and the younger, far prettier, suddenly angry one beside her.

Mary Henderson's mood had undergone the abrupt change because she chose to interpret what Edge said as a subtle slight directed at her. She snapped: 'Far as I'm concerned, there's something you should never have got to taste in Winton, Edge! And you sure won't get a chance to try it again!'

He showed her a smile that gave his thin-lipped mouth an engaging line but failed to bring warmth to the glittering slits of his ice blue eyes. Said as he turned to go toward the doorway and Roxanne drew back off the threshold: 'I recall we had a real satisfying few minutes, ma'am. I'd be a pig to come back for seconds.'

15

He did not try to close the door behind him, for Roxanne
Graham kept firm hold on it as she watched him step out of
René's Place, her flesh-crowded eyes bitterly resentful of him
for not agreeing to do what she and Fletcher Grady had asked
of him.

He paid her no further attention after he tipped his hat to
her, crossed to his horse waiting at the rail. Saw that since she
had reported on the brightly sunlit scene further along Travis
Street, up to and across the intersection with Juniper, it had
ceased to look normal: reverted to the way it had been when
he first peered out of the window at the Winton Hotel,
opened it to widen his view.

The street was deserted and Winton would have been eerily
silent had not the people of the Old Town section continued
to go unobtrusively about their daily business, totally
disinterested in what anybody else in this community was
planning.

As if to underscore the detached attitudes that existed in
this part of town, the fat Marie could be heard softly rasping
harsh-toned words to the two women and the man in her cafe:
surely urging them to leave her establishment, not bring their
trouble here.

Nothing ever is exactly the same as it was before, Edge
reflected as he unhitched the reins to free the once again
uneasy gelding from the rail.

He could see that the shadows of the implacable buildings
along the eastern side of the street were shorter than before,
now the coldly bright sun had dragged itself higher into the
unclouded sky.

When he swung up into the saddle, murmuring softly to the

horse beneath him, stroking the animal's smooth neck, he sensed strongly he was being watched: not only by the sullen-faced trio who filed out of the cafe.

The door was firmly closed at their backs and against the sliding of bolts at the top and bottom, Roxanne asked nervously:

'Where's everybody gone, Goddamnit? They were all over the street awhile ago.'

'It's just like it was when you were at the meeting hall,' Mary told her huskily as, like Roxanne, she and Grady felt compulsively drawn to peer fixedly along the empty, deathly-hushed street. Then she hardened her tone with sneering contempt. 'Some of them getting ready to do something terrible. The rest have locked themselves away: trying to pretend to themselves there's nothing wrong.'

'What d'you think, Mr Edge?' Fletcher Grady asked around the fear that seemed like a palpable blockage in his throat, squinting up at the mounted man silhouetted against the glaringly bright sky: in the same way as Ralph McCloud had done earlier this morning. When the situation had been similar, but nothing was exactly the same as it was now.

Edge did not look down at the man as he backed his horse away from the rail, turned him toward the south and concentrated his narrow-eyed gaze in the same direction. He failed to pinpoint any one place in particular from where he was being watched, and decided there was something else different from before.

Mary Henderson was wrong.

Those citizens of this town who did not intend to involve themselves directly in a new evil had not locked themselves away from it. They were positioned to witness what was about to happen. And the nervous tension of anticipation they experienced as they watched and waited was as powerful as the hostility a lesser number of people directed at the potential victims.

Edge rasped the back of a hand along the bristles on his jawline, growled in response to the frightened Grady: 'I think I could have a little trouble trying to leave town, feller.'

Now it was as if the vocal chords of the duster-coated man

and the two women who flanked him were tightly tied in knots of fear.

The half-breed heeled the horse forward, angled him out on to the centre of the wide street: appeared from a distance to ride with easy nonchalance while his glittering eyes travelled from one side of their sockets to the other under the hooded lids, constantly lengthening and shortening focus as he surreptitiously flexed his muscles, preparing himself to respond to the first sound he heard, sight he saw or anything he sensed that the simmering malevolence within this town was about to erupt into instant violence.

Maybe it was a trick of the imagination or it could have been a fact that the setting down of the gelding's hooves did not sound so loud as Edge rode southward along the centre of Travis Street as when he had come in the opposite direction earlier.

Maybe the street surface had softened, become more resilient on this cold winter day after the hardly discernible warmth of the sun had penetrated deep to unfreeze the earth beneath.

Or, with nobody walking alongside the horse, without whatever protection a deputy's badge provided in a law abiding town like Winton, perhaps a man's mind was concentrated more sharply, and he was more susceptible to every infinitesimal thing that went on around him.

Which, right then, was nothing: outside of his own measured progress, the inching advance of the sun above, the shadows below.

Even Old Town was quiet now, the people who lived there having become aware they could not remain subjectively detached from what was about to happen in the tension-crackling atmosphere of the day that had started with just such a brand of quiet, to be shattered with explosive violence. Or had he simply ridden too far from Old Town for the never clamorous sounds to reach to him against the clop of hooves.

All of which was irrelevant. But none of which he felt able to drive from his mind until the threat of imminent menace became an undeniable reality.

'You goin' someplace in particular, mister?' a man asked

huskily, and stepped out of the mouth of an alley between the Graham Bakery and a candy store to Edge's right.

The half-breed reined in the gelding, stroked the animal's quivering neck, then let his hand rest on his leg inches from the stock of the Winchester that jutted from the forward hung boot. He turned just his head to look at the powerfully built Ernie O'Mally: who stood with legs splayed, a Winchester rifle fisted in a double-handed grip angled across his broad chest.

'I figure where I'm headed is my business, feller,' Edge said, fixed his gaze on the small dark eyes of O'Mally and saw the apprehension in them. He saw, too, the big man had a silver badge pinned to the left side of his topcoat.

'We figure you're the business of the law, Edge,' Bill Henderson said from the other side of the street.

It sounded like he had to make a considerable effort to work toughness into his voice: which acted to defeat the object of the exercise. But when Edge turned his head to look at the doorway of the two-story house immediately opposite the alley mouth where O'Mally stood, he saw the tall and skinny hotel owner was making a better job of manufacturing and sustaining the hard look on his hollow-cheeked, sunken-eyed face.

Henderson's topcoat was open, to display the deputy's badge pinned to his jacket lapel the way McCloud had worn his. With the coat open, it could also be seen that Henderson had a gunbelt slung around his narrow waist. The holster was not tied down, but it was held low by the weight of the Colt which nestled in it and the way Henderson draped a hand firmly over the jutting butt.

'You'll have to explain that, feller,' the half-breed drawled, rested his hand holding the reins on the saddlehorn.

'It's because *I'm* arresting you, sir,' Ralph McCloud announced. He looked precisely the way he sounded when he stepped through one of three doorways of the Winton Theatre on the north west corner of the midtown intersection. He came down the four broad, building wide steps, added: 'Although I prefer to consider I am taking you into protective custody.'

He looked like he had grave doubts about what he was

doing, but was determined to carry it through now that he had persuaded himself to start. He still wore the deputy's badge on his jacket lapel, still looked cold: even more frail than earlier.

'That doesn't explain too much, Doc,' Edge told him.

'He don't like to be called Doc!' Barny Drew snarled, obviously aware he was voicing the same warning Edge had directed at Roy Elrick, a minute before he put a bullet in the drummer's head.

Drew and Shannon had showed themselves at either side of a high thicket of evergreen brush at the front of the vacant lot on the north east corner of the intersection. It was on this lot, Edge recalled as he shifted his impassive gaze back toward the drummers after he saw their abrupt appearance angered McCloud, where Teresa Ward had been raped and murdered: started the chain of events which led to this confrontation. He noted they did not wear badges. If they were armed, they carried concealed weapons.

Then McCloud recaptured all attention when he snarled: 'Henderson! I told you! I'd go along with this only if it was confined to our own people!'

Henderson countered grimly: 'A man like him, Mr Mayor, we need all the help we can get!'

'And we got plenty of help, Edge!' Jeremiah Harman crowed from the roof of the theatre as he stepped from behind the billboard that proclaimed the name of the place, had space beneath to advertise current attractions. Nothing was playing at the theatre right then.

The saloonkeeper had a silver star pinned to his topcoat at the chest. He carried a double-barrel shotgun canted to his shoulder. Held it one handed so he could push a crooked finger and thumb between his lips, vent a shrill whistle.

As the pre-arranged signal sounded, a line of men began to file out from the western length of Juniper, shuffled from the corner of the theatre to the start of the fenced side of the vacant lot opposite.

Some of the warmly clad men wore badges, others did not. More packed holstered handguns than carried rifles canted to their shoulders, angled across their chests or held horizontally across the base of their bellies.

Edge recognised faces from the lynch mob. A few from the fire. Some he could not recall seeing before. Which meant the composition of this group, convinced he had a hand in the series of wanton killings, was far more representative of the town than that which had been ready to string up Grady and Roxanne.

Alvin Ridler was in the line of eighteen men stretched across the intersection to block the half-breed's way south: looked as nervous as most. While a few others, including some storekeepers and a couple of the old-timers who drank in the Oregon Trail, looked a whole lot tougher with less effort than O'Mally and Henderson did: drew comfort and courage from the proximity of others engaged in the same dangerous business.

As the newcomers came to a ragged halt, McCloud cleared his throat, advanced from the foot of the theatre steps, out on to the street toward the man astride the unmoving roan gelding. He halted fifteen feet in front of the horse, cleared his throat again, thrust both hands into the side pockets of his jacket, maybe to hide them in case they began to tremble, as he announced gravely:

'This is absolutely legal, sir.'

'It's a hell of a lot of trouble to go to for spitting in the street,' Edge answered.

'What's that he said, McCloud?' Harman demanded from the theatre roof.

'Can't think of any other local ordinance I might've broken,' Edge told the suddenly scowling old man.

'He's crackin' wise, Jeremiah!' O'Mally called up to Harman.

'You better not treat this so damn easy, mister!' Henderson snarled. He took a few steps away from the open doorway of the house that was one of a line of three fine looking two story frame homes built directly on to the street, separated one from the other by narrow alleys.

'Just as we do not take your threats lightly, sir,' McCloud snapped.

Edge turned in the saddle, surveyed the street behind him.

Saw it was deserted except for Grady and Roxanne who still stood outside the cafe, embracing, while Mary Henderson strode purposefully southward.

'We'd ask you to treat this situation the same,' McCloud completed.

'Threat, Doc?' Edge asked, gazing down at the old man again.

'Precisely, sir! You can see not one man in this legally constituted posse is aiming a firearm at you. This is a sign of our good faith. We are not trying to provoke you to any violent retaliation against what must be done.'

Edge raked his glinting-eyed gaze over the faces of the men ranged against him on three sides. Saw that now the plan had been set in motion, all were able to draw courage from the way they vastly outnumbered their single adversary.

'But I give you fair warning, sir,' McCloud went on. 'If I say the word, every man here will aim and fire at you. That is no idle threat.'

'I reckon my daughter already told you something like this was in the wind?' Henderson asked grimly, cast a malevolent glance toward Mary, who had advanced to within a hundred feet of the confrontation.

'But I didn't realise you had given your blessing to this disgusting lynch mob, Doctor McCloud!' Mary snarled contemptuously at the old man standing in front of Edge.

McCloud winced at the tone of her voice and the substance of what she said. Dragged his gaze away from her to peer up at Edge, shook his head emphatically, insisted: 'That kind of criminal madness is over and done with, sir! I'm arresting you for the suspected murder of Roydon Elrick. You will remain in custody until Sheriff Kenyon returns to investigate the circumstances of that man's death.'

'You honestly think I'm——' Edge started to counter.

McCloud thrust up a hand, then returned it quickly to his pocket, went on: 'Your arrest will also ensure you are kept safely in the jailhouse. Under twenty-four hour guard by depturies sworn to protect you in the event certain hothead elements seek to prejudge the issue.'

He shot a pointed glance toward Drew and Shannon. The

drummers stepped in closer to either side of the thicket, in a way that suggested to Edge guns were hidden within the brush.

'And there's something else, Edge!' O'Malley pointed out. 'If anybody else gets killed while you're in jail, we'll know you ain't the one been doin' all the other——'

'And if the sheriff doesn't come back—and nobody else is murdered—you'll have Edge ready and waiting to string up!' Mary Henderson challenged harshly.

'That madness is over with, I tell you!' McCloud bellowed, his voice rising to a shrill plateau of righteous anger. 'This is a legally sworn posse! If you hand yourself over to us without trouble, Edge, you'll be accorded the full protection of the law. I give you my word.'

Edge once more shifted his glittering-eyed gaze from McCloud to Henderson. Then the drummers flanking the brush. Along the line of men strung across the street. To Harman perched on the theatre roof. Down to O'Mally in the mouth of the alley just as the glowering Mary Henderson moved across the front of Graham's Bakery.

Then he looked back at the frail old man who plainly wished he was someplace else, engaged with his profession as a doctor or the duties of mayor rather than here in the stead of and with the heavy responsibilities of the absent sheriff.

The survey completed, Edge knew he could be within stretched seconds of violent death. Unless there was a miracle, and he did not believe in miracles. Just as he did not believe he could stop himself from submitting to the impulse to speak the thought in his mind and start the move that would invite his bullet-shattering, blood-gouting end.

'Obliged for your word, Doc,' he drawled. 'I've got two for you. But since there's a lady present, I'll just tell you the second one is *off*!'

16

A gunshot cracked through the brittle silence, a shattering exclamation mark that emphasised the force of the implied obscenity.

Jeremiah Harman vented a shriek of shock. Or terror. Or agony. An anguish that encompassed all these feelings.

Edge was the first man on the street to look up at the saloonkeeper on the theatre roof: see the dark stain start to blossom across his coat at the chest. While everyone else stared fixedly at the half-breed, still certain he was about to commit an act of violence in the wake of his retort to McCloud.

But he remained in the saddle, unmoving as his horse except for his head which had turned and tilted to direct his gaze up at the theatre roof. And everyone looked there now, in time to see Harman fling away his shotgun, clutch at his bullet-holed chest with one hand while he reached out to fasten a grip on the billboard with the other.

A moment later he was dead, arms dropped to his sides, then moving through a limp arc as he toppled forward, fell head first to the ground.

He hit the street with a sickening sound of snapping bone.

A second shot cracked out.

Edge wheeled his horse, thudded in his heels to demand an instant gallop. Raced away from where the man who killed Harman was concealed: toward the alley where Ernie O'Mally and Mary Henderson stood, like carved statues, for a moment longer.

Then the woman pressed herself flat to the side wall of the bakery. And O'Mally made to bring his rifle to bear on the half-breed, then threw himself flat to the ground as a fusillade of gunfire exploded.

The roan gelding snorted and stumbled. His rider somehow survived the hail of bullets in which the animal was hit, the side wall of the bakery was splintered and the candy store window was shattered.

But Edge did not entirely escape injury as he kicked his feet free of the stirrups and hurled himself out of the saddle of the tumbling horse. Had no inclination to try to slide the rifle out of the boot as he sought to get clear of crashing horseflesh, hit the ground with a juddering impact that triggered pain to every nerve ending in his body.

He rolled over twice, seeing the changing scenes in a blur. Knew he was giving vent to sounds of pain as his ears were filled with the crackle of more gunfire, the yells of men, the screams of women.

Mary Henderson was not screaming. But she looked like she needed to as she stared down at Edge who had come to rest on his back at her feet. She said to him:

'God, this is so awful!'

'You and me have had better times together,' he rasped through gritted teeth as he sat up, his male pride insisting he suppress the urgent need to give further voice to his hurt while a woman could see and hear him.

But he did not refuse her help to get up. With the hand she did not clutch, reached for Ernie O'Mally's Winchester which the blacksmith had abandoned when he snaked backwards on his belly, desperately seeking to get into the depths of the alley.

Edge shook his head several times as he got to his feet, helped by Mary and the Winchester which he used as a crutch until he was fully erect. This cleared his vision so he could see in sharp focus the inert body of Jeremiah Harman, lying in a crumpled heap at the foot of the theatre steps. Then his gelding, struggling to rise, blood spurting from multiple wounds opened up in one side of his hindquarter.

'I'm obliged, ma'am,' he said, and jerked free of her helping hand. Aimed the Winchester from the hip and blasted a shot into the side of the wounded animal's head.

Two other rifle shots exploded in quick succession. From across the street. Not from the area where the killing shot had been aimed at Harman.

Edge thought he felt the slipstream of one of the bullets across his cheek: maybe only imagined it. Knew for sure he heard the impact of the two bullets: one splintering wood, the other thudding into the dirt at his feet. And Mary certainly vented a startled cry.

Muzzle smoke drifted among the evergreen foliage of the thicket which had been flanked by Drew and Shannon when he last saw the drummers.

There was an instant of silence, then Mary caught her breath and next her footfalls beat on the ground. But she was not retreating deep into the alley where O'Mally had risen into a crouch then pressed himself flat against the wall of the candy store. She had lunged out on to the open street.

Edge glimpsed her on the periphery of his vision as he continued to concentrate his unblinking gaze on the brush at the front of the vacant lot: beyond where Ralph McCloud remained precisely where he stood when the shooting started. But now his hands were clear of his pockets: clapped over his ears. And his eyes were screwed tightly closed as he began to mutter, over and over:

'No, not again. Not in Winton. No, not again. Not in Winton. No, not again——'

The woman's running footfalls were not heavy.

The man's voice was just a rasping whisper.

Then the metallic sounds of the actions of two repeater rifles being pumped, to eject spent cartridges, lever fresh rounds into the breeches, rang out clearly from behind the thicket.

The carcase of the horse involuntarily spasmed as the animal's nervous system finally ceased to function. Edge broke out into a cold sweat as he became sharply aware he could be just as dead: could certainly be so in a matter of moments if he did not duck into cover. Or kill the men who were fully prepared to shoot him down.

He powered forward, hurled down the blacksmith's Winchester. Drew his Colt from the holster in a blur of speed. Dropped into a gunfighter's crouch the instant Ralph McCloud was out of his line of fire to the brush. Levelled the revolver, hooked a finger around the trigger, fanned the hammer with the heel of his free hand.

Like it always did, it hurt his hand to fan the hammer of the big, bucking gun. But not so severely as his whole body suffered from the tumble he took off his doomed horse.

Then the men in back of the brush revealed they hurt more, if the piercing shrillness of their screams were a measure of their pain. They staggered out into the open, both showing on one side of the thicket. Drew and Shannon, banging into each other, spilling blood from several body wounds, their faces contorted by physical agony and the anguish of knowing they were going to die: without even the consolation of avenging the death of their friend.

The Colt was empty.

First Drew, then Shannon, dropped hard to the ground, the impacts spurting blood more forcefully from their wounds.

Silence came once again to Winton that bright, cold, strange morning. For Mary Henderson had gotten to where she was going. And the burst of revolver fire had acted to choke off the repetitious denials of the undeniable truth Ralph McCloud had been voicing.

Edge knew he was still in mortal danger from the people of this town unconcerned with the personal score that had just been settled. And he waited implacably for the death he had expected to be his lot for so many stretched seconds. But instead of another explosion of shots, the new silence was ended by a sob from Mary Henderson.

He turned just his head, fixed his gaze upon the doorway of the house from which her father had emerged. The house out of which the gunshot that killed Jeremiah Harman was fired. And where, under cover of the fusillade that had been loosed to bring down the gelding—might have killed Edge, the woman and O'Mally—another deadly shot exploded. Blasted a bullet into Bill Henderson as he lunged for cover. Sprawled him on his back across the threshold of the house where there was no sanctuary for him.

'This has to stop!' Mary wailed from where she knelt beside her father's corpse, not touching him: turning one fist back

171

and forth in the palm of the other hand, like somebody fighting the impulse to lash out at something or someone. Anything. Anyone.

Edge was about to say something to her. But had not even started to think of what the words would be when somebody yelled:

'Who the frig is that?'

Everybody listened and everybody heard the distant sounds of a two-horse team slowly hauling a wagon along the western stretch of Juniper Street.

One of the men who had scrambled into the cover of the theatre's bulk after the fusillade was fired at Edge yelled in answer to the question: 'It's that army guy come back to town!'

McCloud had gotten a grip on himself: regained enough self-possession to again accept responsibility for the safety of those people in Winton who had taken leave of their senses. He tore his hands down from his head, snapped open his eyes, whirled to bellow across the intersection: 'Tell him to keep his family away from here!'

Then he swung back to glare at Edge, next the two bodies beside the brush, Edge again. Harsh anger contorted his sparsely-fleshed face as the steady clop of hooves and the rattle of turning wheels rose in volume, Lieutenant Nolan drove his rig closer to the intersection.

Nobody complied with McCloud's command.

Everybody was as tense as Edge, waiting for the killing shot to crack out, the half-breed holding the empty Colt to drop to the street, spilling lifeblood. Blasted by the gun that had killed Harman and Bill Henderson. Or from any of those that had been triggered to kill Edge, instead poured lead into his horse.

'It ain't his wife and kids he's got on the wagon!' somebody else called from along the western stretch of Juniper Street. 'It looks like he's... Hell, it is! The lieutenant's haulin' in a couple of corpses!'

'Mister, I——' Ernie O'Mally forced out of a terror-constricted throat as he halted alongside Edge. Scanned the street on which McCloud, Mary Henderson and the half-

172

breed all stood, seemingly immune to gunfire. 'It looks like we got it all wrong!'

'Everyone makes mistakes,' Edge growled tautly, responding to the blacksmith but gazing fixedly at McCloud. Whose expression changed from malevolence to confusion, then to something akin to shame as Edge went on, 'I heard Henderson was on the John Grady jury. The saloonkeeper, too?'

'No, Harman wasn't, but he was one of them would've lynched Curly Grady,' Alvin Ridler said as he emerged from behind the fence at the side of the vacant lot.

'Who you got wrapped in the blankets, Lieutenant?' a man called.

'Papers on them say they're Miss Helen Cannon and Vernon Bassett,' Nolan answered as he rolled the flatbed wagon to a halt at the point where Juniper Street reached the intersection. 'Found them shot in the head at the side of the trail five miles west of town. These were around their necks.'

With each hand he picked up a noose off the seat beside him. As mass shocked attention was focused on the circles of rope, he swept his gaze from the bodies of the two drummers to that of Henderson, then Harman and the carcase of the horse. He shook his head, admitted in a dull tone:

'Figured when I heard the gunfire I was probably too late to make any difference.'

'Miss Mary, don't go in there!' O'Mally implored, drew all attention away from the wagon toward the slender, quietly sobbing young woman as she rose to her feet, turned to enter the house.

'Kenyon won't kill her, feller,' Edge said.

'What?' The query was croaked by Ralph McCloud.

'She didn't have anything to do with the Grady boy getting——'

McCloud insisted in a stronger tone: 'You said the sheriff!'

A voice Edge did not recognise sneered disdainfully: 'Shit, just because that's his house don't mean he——'

Mary Henderson screamed.

So did her mother, who was one of the throng of people who had emerged on to the streets of Winton in the wake of

173

what had seemed to be the end of this new explosion of violence.

But the two screams acted to halt the mass advance, stunned everyone into unmoving silence.

Edge acted instinctively. Maybe recklessly: but not totally unthinkingly. He knew the Colt was empty of live rounds as he thrust it back in his holster. Knew he could have stooped, slid his Winchester out of the boot of the saddle on the dead horse.

But he bet his life he had no need of a weapon to defend himself as he strode across the street toward the house. Reached the spreadeagled body of Bill Henderson with a blood-crusted bullet hole in the centre of his chest just as the dead man's daughter appeared at the doorway: to prove he had been right to think the way he did before he started his move.

She acted like a sleepwalker as her lips moved to speak softly to Edge words that could not reach more distant ears straining to learn what she said.

'Sheriff Kenyon killed my father?'

It was a question spoken with a sense of incredulity as she staggered, sagged against the doorframe. But then she got a grip on herself, assured Edge as he reached a hand out toward her: 'I'm all right. He killed all those people?'

Edge moved into the house, leaving Mary to remain on the threshold, peering down at her father.

Footfalls sounded on the streets of Winton as its citizens advanced without haste on the house of Sheriff Nicholas Kenyon.

Just one of the doors leading off the longer than it was wide entrance hallway was open. It gave on to a room at the rear of the house, to the right.

Edge went toward it, halted on the threshold of a bachelor's inner sanctum. A thickly carpeted room furnished with dark and heavy pieces counterpointed by polished glass and the gleaming brass of lamps. There were display cases filled with handguns and rifles, a collection of lawmen's badges and some scrolls that doubtless recorded honours achieved by a proud man. One wall was taken up by floor to ceiling bookcases lined with leather bound volumes. The wall opposite was hung with ornately framed portraits of stern-faced, learned-looking men.

'I lived my life by the letter of the law, Edge,' the stern-faced but not so learned-looking Kenyon said in a monotone from where he sat in a large leather chair behind a large oak, leather topped desk across from the doorway. With the hand not holding his revolver he motioned to encompass his surroundings. 'All this is concerned with the honourable profession of jurisprudence. Little of it having any direct relevance to me, unfortunately. Or maybe fortunately, the way events have conspired against me.'

His revolver lay on the leather bound blotter in front of him, loosely held in his unmoving hand.

'Because I sent an innocent young man to unjust execution,' he went on in the same carefully dispassionate way. 'Not me alone, of course. So many people of this once fine town had a hand in doing that. But I have made some restitution, I figure. Judge Benedict. Some of the jury members. The O'Hara brothers and that bigot Harman who'd tried him in the newspaper and the saloon even before he came to court.'

He sighed, shook his head, looked down at the hand clasping the gun butt. 'I'd hope to do more. But it had to end before other innocent victims suffered. And it's almost enough to make this town think real hard before they send anyone else to the gallows unless...'

Edge had listened impassively to the man whom he felt sure was a little or totally insane. And he remained impassive in the doorway as the lawman opened a drawer, took out a rope noose and set it down on the blotter. Then raised the Colt, pushed the muzzle into his mouth beneath the blond moustache, thumbed back the hammer and squeezed the trigger.

The back of his head was blasted open and had he been seated in a less sturdily made chair he would probably have been tipped over backwards by the force of the shot at point blank range. But after his shattered head slammed against the back of the chair, he jerked forward and tipped sideways.

When he was inertly slumped over the arm of his chair and the acrid taint of black powder smoke had been neutralised by the chill air, Edge went to the door, looked down into the open drawer. Saw two more ready-made nooses were stored in there, along with a coil of rope from which many more could have been fashioned.

He turned then and left the room. Left the house and saw a mass of people were gathered into a large half circle on the street from which the human corpses had been removed. They all peered at him with funereal expressions.

'Where does a feller buy a horse in this town?' he asked.

'The sheriff?' Ralph McCloud asked, his voice hardly audible, as he took an unlit cigar out of his mouth.

'Mrs Crocker'll be takin' care of the business now Delmar's dead,' Fletcher Grady told Edge.

He and Roxanne were tightly holding hands instead of embracing now.

'That gunshot?' McCloud demanded, forceful now. 'What happened? Is Nicholas..?'

'He was the killer, Doc,' the half-breed told him as he started across the street to get his gear off his dead horse.

The crowd, from which Mary Henderson and her mother were missing, parted to allow him through.

'He killed all those people and then he—' McCloud couldn't finish what he started.

'He had a powerful sense of guilt, Doc,' Edge said. 'And he had plenty of rope. But like you heard, he didn't hang himself.'